JODY SAVAGE

Shadows on the Road

For Motivated Savages: the dreamers, the doers, the ones who refuse to fade into the shadows.

Some shadows aren't cast by light,
but by the weight of what's been left
behind.

Contents

Preface

This story began with a single image: a lone cyclist disappearing into the fog along the Maine coast. I did not know their name or destination, only that they were riding through something heavier than the mist itself. It was not weather pressing down on them. It was memory.

From that image grew Havenport, a town shaped by silence and superstition, and the people who carry both. Some of them walk through shadows. Some of them become them. All of them are searching for light in their own way.

Writing this book was like following an unmarked road at dusk. The path was winding, uncertain, and beautiful. It asked me to keep going even when I could not see the end, to trust the next turn, and to let the story reveal itself at its own pace.

To everyone who keeps going when the way ahead is unclear, and to all the Motivated Savages who choose to rise again and again, this one is for you.

— *Jody Savage*

Acknowledgments

Writing this book was both a solitary journey and a shared one. While the hours were spent alone with words, I was never truly alone.

Thank you to Amanda and Toni, who stepped into this story before it was fully formed and offered their honest eyes and steady encouragement. Your belief helped me see what it could become.

Thank you to the friends who asked about this novel when it was only scattered notes and late-night whispers, and who celebrated every small milestone along the way.

And to my Maine roots, with their fog, quiet backroads, and small towns that carry more stories than they let on, thank you for shaping the soul of this book.

Finally, to every reader who turns these pages: your time and trust mean everything. I hope this story lingers with you, just as it has lingered with me.

— *Jody Savage*

I

Silent Shadows

1

Fog of Shadows

Before dawn, Havenport lay buried beneath a heavy October fog. It pressed inland from the sea, thick and relentless, like a secret too heavy to hold. The town had vanished beneath it. Narrow streets blurred into shadows, tall pines faded to silhouettes, and even the familiar became strange.

Waves murmured against the shore, their sound low and muffled, a hollow pulse rising from somewhere beyond. The ocean, once familiar and soothing, offered no comfort this morning.

The streets were empty. The silence wasn't still; it breathed. It moved through the alleyways and rooftops, wrapping around fences and mailboxes. It whispered. Not loud, not clear, but enough. Old stories, maybe. Half-truths. Secrets the town had buried long ago.

Then, slicing through the stillness, came movement.

Derek Marshall surged forward, pedaling hard, his neon jersey a sharp streak against the gray. Tall and lean, his frame shaped by countless hours on the bike, muscles built through early morning climbs along winding hills.

To most, these roads felt overwhelming. But not to Derek. For him, they were a way of life. Each climb and descent tested his control and endurance. Cycling wasn't just exercise. It was his escape. The path ahead and the power in his legs were all that mattered. And nothing, not even the damp chill of a Maine autumn, could interfere with that.

His life followed a strict routine. Mornings were for riding, afternoons for running the hardware store on Main Street, and evenings reserved for calm dinners, stretching, and rest. Every day, predictable and precise.

Pushing harder, he was determined to shake off the fatigue and settle back into his zone. With a controlled breath, he surged forward, wheels spinning on the slick pavement as dread crept in. He tried to ignore it, focusing on his usual mantra: *pedal, breathe, push forward.*

Halfway up Snake Hollow's long climb, a flash of color broke through the clouded air. A lone cyclist came into view, riding downhill, in the opposite direction. They were not managing it well. The rider's posture was tense, wobbling as their tires cut uneven lines along the wet road. They looked back once, uncertain or afraid.

Derek shifted slightly, his cadence slowing. He could have

called out, asked if they were all right. A quick turnaround, and he could catch them easily. The whole thing would take less than a minute.

But he didn't.

Instead, he dipped his head and kept going, offering a small nod as they passed each other. The rider didn't respond.

Just new to the roads, he told himself. People get spooked on these hills all the time. It didn't mean anything. The image stayed with him, the way they looked back, the uneven lines their tires had drawn. Something about it bothered him, not enough to stop, but enough to wonder.

He pushed harder, settling into the pace that always carried him forward. The road kept rising, but Derek no longer felt in control. Not completely.

The path was narrow and steep, lined with stretched-out pines. The heavy morning air muffled everything, even the faint rustle of branches. A sudden chill crept over him, biting at his skin. Each corner seemed darker than he remembered.

Goosebumps rose on Derek's arms. He adjusted his grip on the handlebars and told himself it was just his mind playing tricks. Then came a sound. A low, faint noise drifted through the stillness. His heart began to race as he strained to hear, but the sound had vanished.

He pushed forward, trying to shake the creeping dread. Each

breath came sharp, his muscles burning as the incline steepened. His awareness narrowed, straining to make out the road ahead. The summit had to be close, yet it remained hidden.

He drew a sharp breath as he scanned the roadside, an icy feeling settled in his stomach. Clinging to the motion, he forced the rising fear back down. He didn't know what was coming, but that had never stopped him before.

Something took shape in the mist. Low to the ground, it stretched across the road. A small, dark object that didn't belong. He slowed, instinct kicking in. A broken spoke, jagged and twisted. Like it had been waiting for him.

His heart stuttered as fear shot through his chest. He braked hard. Tires skidded against the wet pavement, hissing beneath him. The bike shuddered to a stop. Derek stared at the spoke, his breath short and sharp. Just a piece of metal, discarded and meaningless to most. But not to him. Not to anyone who knew what it meant.

To the outside world, it was trash. To a cyclist, it was a warning. He should have kept going, should have kept climbing like he had a hundred times before. But the spoke held him.

He exhaled hard, trying to shake the unease climbing his spine. He forced his feet down on the pedals, pushing forward with a speed that felt like defiance. The mist closed in again. Trees blurred, and the road narrowed. For the first time in years, Derek Marshall didn't know where he was. Not on the map, or in his mind.

Another sound caught his attention. A faint rustle, just above the whisper of his tires. He slowed, scanning. Maybe it was the wind, or nothing at all, yet something in it tightened his nerves.

His heart thudded as he looked back. He told himself it was a deer or a fox. Something simple and harmless. But he knew better; his body had already made that clear.

He eased his speed again, coasting toward a curve in the road. Shapes flickered at the edge of his vision; too quick to name, too still to dismiss. Was it the wind stirring the trees, or something watching just beyond the light?

For one breathless second, he thought he saw someone. The air changed. It happened fast, like the pressure drop before a storm. Derek spun, his bike wobbling beneath him. A shape emerged, cutting the distance between them.

Impact, swift and clean. He hit the ground hard, the bike skidding away. Pain shot through his ribs. A boot slammed against his chest, pinning him in place. There was no urgency in the movement. Only precision, complete control.

He looked up into a pair of eyes. Cold and piercing. No panic; pure intent. A bitter scent drifted through the air, faint but sharp. Dry and smoky, it clung to the cold. He drew in a quick breath. He had smelled it before. Not often, but enough to unsettle him.

Something tightened inside him, not from pain, but recognition. His mind could not place it, but his body already had. Panic surged. The figure didn't flinch. There was no rage. No hesitation. Only the practiced stillness of someone who had done this before.

A flash of light caught his attention; small, sharp, and familiar. A broken spoke, held like a weapon. Poised and certain, meant for this moment.

Derek barely had time to react before it struck. The metal tore into his side. Pain exploded. His body jerked as blood poured freely, soaking his jersey and seeping into the cold road beneath him. The chill had vanished, replaced by a sickening warmth that spread through his core.

His vision blurred as shapes twisted. The world around him faded. The figure above him didn't speak or rush, simply watched.

As his strength drained, the pressure on his chest lifted. He collapsed fully onto the road. The cold crept back in. The attacker knelt beside him, placing the broken spoke next to his body, like an offering.

They stood and turned with deliberate grace. A final glance over the shoulder and then gone. The trees swallowed them, the fog erasing the trail behind.

His final awareness came not in sight or sound, but in feeling. The helplessness. The truth, settling in his chest like a stone.

Deep within the pines, a crow's harsh call shattered the quiet. Its cry carried an indifference, a reminder that nature acknowledged the violence. The sound faded, leaving the woods hushed once more. The figure paused one last time, the town's murmurs barely reaching through the trees. The work wasn't done; there were still roads to haunt.

The faint chime of a church bell rang out. It marked the passing of another hour. While the forest held its breath, the town exhaled. Life moved forward as energy pulsed through Havenport, alive with excitement and edged with apprehension.

The "Havenport Classic" was on everyone's minds, bold posters plastered across weathered storefronts: *This Saturday: The Race is on!*

Despite the recent events, the annual race remained a powerful draw, a strange blend of hope and distraction, tradition and denial.

The Haven Café was busy this morning, filled with the nervous chatter of locals and cyclists. The warm scent of freshly brewed coffee and cinnamon pastries mixed with the salty breeze drifting in through the open windows.

Conversations centered on strategies, favorite routes, and predictions about who might win. Cyclists in neon jerseys added splashes of color to the wooden chairs and tables. The bright colors stood out against the somber mood.

Ryan Moore stepped inside, shrugging off his jacket. He was greeted with nods and waves. Some welcomed him with casual ease, and others had a hint of hesitation. Ryan offered an easy smile as he scanned the room. His presence remained magnetic, even with the suspicion hanging over the entire cycling community.

He moved through the crowd and leaned casually against the counter. He searched until his eyes landed on Lena Crawford. She was swirling her spoon absently in her coffee.

Ryan approached her. There was a curious edge to his words. "Feeling the jitters?"

Lena glanced up. "Maybe a little," she admitted. "It's not like I haven't raced here before, but this year feels different."

Ryan nodded thoughtfully. "More pressure," he said. "More people are watching. You've been winning more. You've got a reputation now."

Lena sighed, her fingers tapping lightly on the table's edge. "It's not about winning. I need to prove myself, as much to me as to everyone else."

Ryan's tone softened. "I get that. There's a thrill to winning. The real challenge is inside. It's about pushing past the limits you thought were there."

Lena's lips curled into a weak smile. "You sound like Marissa. She used to say the same thing. It wasn't about beating others.

It was about beating herself."

Ryan smiled faintly. "That sounds like her. She was always in a race of her own, even when she was miles ahead of the rest of us."

They sat together, the low hum of the café filling the space between them.

Lena looked toward the window. "Do you think Marissa ever watches us and feels... lost? Like she's here, but not really part of it anymore?"

Ryan followed her line of sight, drawn to the blurred reflections of town life outside. "I think she's proud in her own way. But it's different now. The shop, the tools, and the repairs; that's her race now."

Lena inched forward. "She was such a force. How do you go from that to... this?" She gestured vaguely, struggling to explain the ache of watching someone so fierce become so still.

Ryan didn't answer right away. He remained turned toward the window, his thoughts drifting.

"I should've said something," he murmured at last. "Back when everything started slipping. I saw it. How much she was carrying, how hard she was pushing. We all did. But I stayed out of it. I told myself it wasn't my place, figured she wouldn't listen anyway. But the truth is, I didn't even try."

Lena was still, watching him.

"She never really bounced back," he said. "It wasn't just the injury or being left behind. We all let her fade out."

Lena stared into her coffee, still stirring slowly. "She didn't totally disappear. She's still around and tied to all of this."

Ryan nodded. "She didn't leave, but she's not here either. What's left is someone who's just trying to get through the day."

Lena hesitated. "Do you think she's bitter?"

He didn't flinch. "She's bitter, alright. But it's not just about the races. It's about losing herself. And I don't blame her."

There was another pause. Then Lena spoke. "Lately, I've started wondering... what happens when it's me?"

Ryan blinked. "What do you mean?"

She stared at her coffee. "When does it stop being fun? When does it become something I keep doing because everyone expects me to? Because I expect it?"

She looked up. "What if I push too hard and something snaps... and I don't even see it coming?"

Ryan leaned back slightly, studying her. "Lena, you're one of the toughest riders out there."

"I know," she said. "And that's the problem. Nobody expects someone like me to question any of it. But I do."

Her voice faltered, then steadied. "I love the ride. I love the wind in my chest and the ache in my legs. But sometimes I think… what if that love changes and I don't notice until it's too late?"

He didn't rush to reassure her. He let it sit.

"You'd notice," he said eventually. "Because you're paying attention. That's what makes you different."

She met his stare, then nodded slowly. "I hope so."

Ryan offered the smallest smile. "Maybe Marissa wasn't the only one racing herself."

Lena sat back and folded her arms. "Maybe. Or we're all just running from the same thing and pretending it's a finish line."

As Ryan absorbed her words, the café door creaked open. Nessa Greene stepped inside, her long, dark coat brushing the floor behind her. Damp auburn hair clung to her pale face, and her sharp green eyes swept the room with a strange intensity.

The café's lively chatter seemed to halt at her entrance, and a ripple of discomfort spread through the crowd.

Ryan stiffened. "Here comes Havenport's resident ghost," he muttered.

Lena shot him a curious glance. "She always seems out of place here. I've never understood what keeps her here."

Ryan stared at Nessa, "She's always been an outsider, but I don't think she's leaving anytime soon. Whatever she's searching for, she hasn't found it yet."

Nessa's attention landed on Ryan and Lena. Her lips curved into a faint smile. She slowly walked over, savoring the mood she created.

"Well, well," Nessa murmured, with a strange, haunting tone. "The stars of Havenport, holding court like it's the Tour de France."

Lena barely looked up. "What do you want, Nessa?"

"Nothing," Nessa shrugged. "Just watching. Funny how you all keep riding like the roads were made just for you."

Ryan's jaw tightened. "We ride because we enjoy it, Nessa. It's that simple."

Nessa's face changed. "Simple? Maybe to you. Tell that to the folks stuck behind five of you on a blind turn in the rain. Or when you fly past, like the rules don't apply."

Lena took a deep breath, holding her ground. "We are careful and follow the rules. We're not reckless."

Nessa's smile was paper-thin. "You're careful. Always careful.

Yet somehow, the bodies keep stacking up."

Ryan's hand curled into a fist against the table. "You don't know what you're talking about."

Nessa leaned in slightly. "I know exactly what I'm talking about. The road doesn't play favorites. It remembers and it punishes."

She let the words sit before turning toward the counter. "Anyway. Don't mind me. "Just passing through."

She moved off without saying another word, ordering her usual tea from Marie, who kept her eyes politely down.

"I just don't get it," Nessa said, nodding toward the cyclists. "Out there in this soup like it's nothing. You'd think they're trying to get hit."

Marie didn't look up, just kept preparing the tea with her usual calm.

"And the way they take up the whole road," Nessa added, shaking her head. "Try getting past one of those packs when you're already running late. It's a nightmare."

Marie gave a polite nod, saying nothing.

Nessa leaned in a little. "And the stop signs? Might as well be suggestions. They blow right through 'em. Like the rules don't apply."

Marie handed over the tea without a word. Nessa went silent for a second. She looked back toward Lena. She was laughing at something Ryan said, her body loose with confidence, her hand still wrapped around her coffee mug like the world couldn't touch her.

"That girl," Nessa nodded. "Lena."

She stared for a moment too long. "She reminds me of someone."

Marie finally glanced up. "Who?"

Nessa blinked like she was caught off guard. Her throat tightened around the words. "Me," she said. "A long time ago."

Her voice cracked on the last word.

"She's got that fire in her legs," she continued, forcing a shrug. "Same wild look I had."

She stopped and cleared her throat. "Anyway," she muttered. "Doesn't matter."

She pushed the door open with her shoulder, her coat sweeping behind her.

Ryan and Lena exchanged a look. Cyclists have become a symbol of friction, of roads disturbed and routines interrupted. Nessa's dark presence deepened the question no one dared to ask. Was it all bad luck, or was there someone watching?

Lena let out a slow breath. "She gives me the creeps. Like she's part of the fog somehow."

Ryan gave a half nod. "She never misses a chance to take a shot at us. Always some weird warning buried in her words."

Lena rubbed her arms. "It's not just hate. It's like she thinks we don't belong here. Like the roads are hers."

She looked at him. "You think she's dangerous or just playing some twisted game?"

Ryan crossed his arms, gazing out the window. "I used to think it was just Nessa being... Nessa. Eccentric. Bitter. But lately..."

2

The Arrival

Detective Claire Sandoval's car crawled along the narrow curves of Snake Hollow. There was a sting in the morning air. The tall trees on either side stood straight up, their branches swaying gently in the breeze.

She cracked the window, and the cool air slipped in. Even with the sun now risen, it struggled to break through the overcast sky.

The road twisted beneath the evergreens, winding deeper into the trees. It didn't feel like a route to a crime scene. It felt like crossing into another realm: calm, watchful, and frozen in time.

Claire gripped the wheel tightly. She knew the feeling by now; that slow build, the pressure that came with getting close to whatever truth waited ahead. She rounded the final bend, and there they were. Blue and red lights, pulsing ahead. A knot tightened deep in her chest.

She pulled off to the shoulder, tires crunching over wet gravel. As she stepped out, her boots sank into the soaked ground. She pulled her coat tighter. The air bit at her skin while the scent of pine hung thick, laced with the faint, unmistakable tang of blood.

Claire scanned the scene, her expression unreadable. The victim lay sprawled across the pavement, his neon cycling jersey torn, stained deep red. Nearby, his bike was on its side, one wheel turning in slow, aimless circles.

Sergeant Ben Foster spotted her and walked over, his boots leaving wide prints on the pavement. He moved like someone used to sad news. Fifty-something, broad-shouldered, with a face that had seen too much. He gave Claire a grim nod.

"Morning, Sandoval. It's Derek Marshall."

Claire didn't respond right away. All she saw was the body, sprawled beside the roadside. The twisted spoke glinted just beyond his hand, angled with care.

"One stab wound?" she asked.

Ben nodded. "Lower abdomen. Same depth. Same angle. The spoke was right here when we got on scene. It hasn't moved."

Claire crouched low; the cold water seeping into her slacks went unnoticed. The wound was sharp. Clean and deliberate. No sign of rage or panic..

Her breath came out slowly. "This wasn't sloppy," she said. "It was precise. Like the others."

Ben shifted beside her. "If this is the same killer, that makes four in as many weeks."

Claire didn't look up. "It is the same killer."

He didn't speak, just watched her. She stood slowly and scanned the tree line, the empty stretch of road curling out of sight.

"They're not killing for chaos," she continued. "They're choosing. Curating fear, one victim at a time."

Ben's jaw clenched. "Derek wasn't flashy. Rode the same loop every morning. Didn't have beef with anyone I ever heard of."

Claire nodded absently. "And Victor kept his distance. Respected, but cold. Elliot was hot-headed and reckless. He was always drawing attention. Megan was different, though; she held people together. Made things better just by being there."

Her voice hushed. "Now, Derek. Always composed and so reliable."

Ben raised an eyebrow. "They're not exactly the same type."

"No," Claire said. "They were not chosen for the same reasons. Whoever's doing this... she's choosing them for how they shape the world around them. For the space they take up."

Ben caught the word. "She?"

Claire didn't flinch. "Yeah. I think it's a woman."

There was a pause. Ben didn't move. "You're basing that on the wounds?" he asked, carefully.

"And the pattern, control, and the pace. The way she walks away like she belongs here. No panic. No trace. It's like she's not even hiding. Just... fading."

Ben raised a brow. "Or maybe he's just smart enough to make it look like that."

Claire turned to him, her words measured. "She's not trying to blend in. She already does. We're not looking outside the cycling world. We're looking inside it."

He looked away, jaw tight, and let out a loud sigh. "My niece rides out here."

Claire blinked. He rarely mentions family.

"She's twenty. College kid. Rides these same backroads, training for a charity ride."

He shook his head. "She's not part of the scene like these others, but still, you start seeing spoke patterns next to bodies, and it stops being just another case."

Claire's voice softened slightly. "That's why we have to find her. Whoever she is, she's not done."

Ben nodded, slowly. "Just make sure we're not building a profile to fit a hunch. We need to make this community safe again."

Claire turned back towards the body. "This isn't a hunch."

Ben didn't argue. But he didn't agree either.

"We need to go deeper," she said. "Look closer at their lives. These weren't random targets. There's a pattern. It's just buried under reputation and routine."

Ben's voice was even. "Then we'd better start looking at who knows how to disappear in plain sight."

She crouched again. The spoke gleamed up at her.

The sound of footsteps on wet gravel broke her concentration. Claire turned.

Ryan Moore approached, tall and confident, his silhouette clearly defined against the morning light. He wore tight-fitting cycling gear; his jacket zipped up, and his padded leggings were still damp from the ride.

There was a rawness to him. He looked like someone shaped by the hard coastlines, built for endurance, and comfortable with being alone.

Claire stepped toward him, intercepting before he got too close to the body.

"Detective Sandoval," Ryan greeted her with an edge of urgency. "I came as soon as I heard."

She couldn't deny the pull toward Ryan, a mixture of curiosity and caution that made her both intrigued and wary. "How did you hear so quickly?"

He hesitated, then shrugged. "It's the fourth cyclist in four weeks. News like that travels fast."

She watched him, weighing his presence, his words. Ryan always had a way of walking the line between sincerity and secrecy. "Any thoughts on this one?"

Ryan glanced past her, toward the edge of the scene, then looked away. "Not about Derek, exactly. But... Lena and I saw Nessa this morning at the Haven Café. And it didn't feel like a coincidence."

Claire's posture shifted. "What happened?"

"She walked up to us like she'd been waiting," he said. "Didn't seem angry, just off. She went on about cyclists again. Said we act like we own the roads. But this time, there was something behind it. Like she meant more than what she said."

Claire stayed, listening.

"Then she said the roads test people. That not everyone makes it back." He looked at her, unsure. "Sounded like nonsense. But there was more to it. Like a warning."

"And Lena?" Claire asked.

"Didn't say much. But I could tell it got to her. Nessa looked at her like she expected her to understand."

He lowered his voice. "She talks about the deaths like they're inevitable. Like they make sense in some twisted way."

He paused, glancing toward the trees. "She's holding something back. I'm sure of it."

Claire nodded slowly. "She's always had a strange way of seeing the world. But if her tone has changed, that's worth paying attention to."

Ryan exhaled. "I figured you'd want to know. Even if it only confirms what you're already thinking."

Claire gave a small, knowing smile. "Sometimes the ones who talk in riddles are the ones closest to the truth."

She placed a hand lightly on his arm, a gesture that surprised even her. "Thanks for bringing it to me. Head home and get some rest. I'll be in touch."

Ryan nodded. "Anytime, Claire."

As he turned to walk away, Claire watched him go, not ready to look away. He still carried a piece of the puzzle, but never the whole picture. That part hadn't changed.

The road stretched ahead. Morning light filtered through the branches, but the weight across Claire's shoulders didn't lift; it clung to her.

The image stayed sharp in her mind: the broken spoke beside the body, the damp air rolling over the pavement, the precision of the wound. But beneath it all, something stirred deeper. Not the crime, a memory.

Years ago, there had been a string of overdoses in a coastal town like Havenport. The cases had come across her desk; young, scattered deaths tied up with clean paperwork and vague conclusions. A coincidence, they said. No signs of foul play. Claire had followed the evidence, closed the files, and moved on.

But her gut hadn't. It had whispered the same thing it did now, that something didn't sit right.
There had been a grieving mother who begged her to look again. Who said her daughter hadn't just slipped away. That she'd been afraid of something, or someone. Claire hadn't listened.

Two months later, another death. Then a new detective picked up the case Claire had walked away from. And the mother's eyes, when she learned her daughter might have been the first and not the last, Claire never forgot them.

She'd promised herself that she wouldn't do that again. Not this time.

Claire got into her car and drove off; the broken spoke fixed in her mind. Main Street came into view, with painted trim and potted plants, neat sidewalks, and small comforts. The illusion of normalcy brushed up against her thoughts. Kids pedaled past on bikes. A shopkeeper arranged fresh flowers outside her door. The town wore its routine like armor.

She could feel it under the surface: tension, still and waiting. Something had crept in. She tightened her grip on the wheel. This time, she wouldn't look away. She wasn't just chasing a killer; she was chasing a second chance.

A few blocks away, the door to Grayson's Bike Shop swung open with a cheerful jingle.

Liam Harper stepped inside. The place buzzed with weekend energy; kids gathered near the back, admiring their freshly tuned bikes, their laughter rising above the low murmur of conversation.

The shop felt like its own small world, untouched by what waited just beyond the trees. But Liam wasn't there to warm up. He wasn't even sure he was here to write. He was chasing something, athread that had started to feel more like responsibility than a headline.

The paper might call him a reporter, but lately, the title didn't fit. What he did wasn't about quotes and headlines anymore. It was about bearing witness, listening to what wasn't said.

As Liam made his way through the shop, he found Sarah Connolly. She stood by the cluttered workbench, flipping through a catalog with Jasper Grayson. Both carried the look of locals who had seen too much and were determined to make sense of the recent tragedies.

As Liam opened his mouth to greet them, Sarah looked up. Her face fell slightly.

"Liam." The name slipped from her lips. "You heard about Derek, didn't you? They found him this morning in Snake Hollow."

The words hit him square in the chest. He swallowed, his mind struggling to process it. "Derek? Not Derek. I thought he was…"

He trailed off, unable to finish the sentence. Derek had been the dependable one. The bridge between generations. The man who kept showing up for people even after the joy started slipping from their rides.

Jasper, tinkering with a set of gears, glanced up. Sadness creased his face. "Yeah, it's true. Another rider gone. If you're here for the story you were working on… well, Derek was a big part of it, Liam. More than a name on the list."

Liam took a breath, pulling out his notebook. "I wanted to write in a way that honored them. Victor, Elliot, Megan… and now Derek. They were more than victims. They were the ones people counted on. I need to capture that."

Jasper leaned back on his stool, voice low. "Victor was sharp. Always studying people, figuring out how they moved, where they slipped. He rode like it was a game of chess. Megan? She was the heart of it all. She pulled people in. Started rides, coached kids, and organized charity events. Made cycling feel like home."

Sarah added gently, "And Derek... he was the glue, Liam. Kept everyone going when the losses piled up. He was calm and unwavering. If Victor was the head and Megan the heart, Derek was the rhythm."

Liam scribbled their words with care. This wasn't filler. This was the center of the story. And now, it was unraveling.

He looked up. "What about Elliot? He always felt different. Like he was chasing something none of us could see."

On cue, the door chimed again. Tommy Reyes stepped inside. His usual confidence dimmed, shoulders tight beneath his hoodie. He gave a cautious nod toward the group.

"Tommy," Liam greeted him. "Good timing. I wanted to ask you about Elliot."

"What do you want to know?" Tommy asked.

Liam kept his voice even. "Elliot was obsessed with the Ghost Rider. I need to know if that was talk, or if it was real."

Tommy exhaled. "It was real. At least, it felt that way. We were out on a night ride; me, Elliot, and a couple of others. Then this guy appears outta nowhere. Black bike, no lights, and fast. Too fast."

He paused, jaw tightening. "It wasn't just that he passed you. It was how. Like he was making a point. Like you didn't belong on the road."

Sarah leaned in. "Did Elliot ever confront him?"

"He tried once," Tommy said. "Got close enough to yell. The Ghost Rider didn't respond. Just looked back, then picked up speed as if it were a game. Elliot kept chasing. Kept trying to prove something."

Jasper's voice was grim. "If that's true... maybe the broken spoke isn't symbolic. Maybe it's more."

Liam's pulse quickened. He flipped a page in his notebook. "So, the spoke could be the Ghost Rider's way of staking a claim?"

Tommy nodded. "It wasn't about winning. It was about breaking them down. Elliot wasn't chasing him; he was running from something darker."

A silence fell before Sarah asked, "Do you think Megan knew? Maybe she was trying to protect Elliot?"

Tommy looked away. "She warned him. Told him to stop looking in the dark for answers. She knew something. I'm sure of it."

Liam paused. The Ghost Rider wasn't just a myth whispered on damp trails. And the broken spoke wasn't just a message; it was growing sharper with each loss.

"Tommy," he said, "if the Ghost Rider is real, there has to be someone else who's seen him."

Tommy hesitated, then said, "The coastal road, near the lighthouse. That's where people say he shows up. It was where Elliot had his worst crash and where Victor said he saw someone watching from the trees."

As Liam noted this, a group of kids near the back of the shop shifted. They'd been listening the whole time. One of them, lanky and pale with windburned cheeks, stepped forward.

"Mr. Harper," Max began. "I don't know if this means anything. We think Derek was trying to warn Ryan... well, before this happened."

Liam paused, intrigued. "What do you mean, Max?"

The other teens nodded as Max continued, gathering his thoughts. "Last week, Derek pulled Ryan aside after our ride. He looked... serious. More serious than normal."

Max's face was etched with worry as he stared at Liam. "We didn't hear much. He sounded scared. Like he sensed things were about to go wrong."

Another rider, a girl with short red hair, spoke up. "Derek kept talking about how things weren't what they seemed, and he told Ryan that he needed to be careful. Like, wicked careful."

A chill twisted in Liam's chest as he took in their words. "So, Derek thought Ryan might be next?" he asked.

Max nodded. "We think he did. He was worried Ryan would end up like the others. And when we tried asking him about it, he shook his head, like he didn't want us in the middle of it. It was like he was protecting Ryan... or trying to."

Tommy, who had been listening intently, crossed his arms. "If Derek thought Ryan was in danger, he would've said something. He wouldn't let that slide. Maybe he was starting to put it together. Or he saw something out there."

Liam took in their words, his pulse jumping. This wasn't just about piecing together lives for a feature. It was about understanding why these people were being targeted. With each death, a darker pattern was forming. Whatever Derek had uncovered hadn't just shaken him. It had cost him his life.

Liam wasn't just reporting; he is part of it now. The line between observer and participant had blurred, and the story was pulling him in whether he liked it or not.

He'd always trusted the facts and let them speak. But this was different. The danger felt close, the truth urgent. If he hesitated and played it safe, someone else might end up like Derek.

The story was no longer waiting. Neither could he.

"Thank you for telling me," Liam said. "It matters more than you know."

The group of young riders nodded with a mix of fear and gratitude on their faces.

With a final look at Jasper and Sarah, Liam tucked his notebook away and headed for the door. He walked out into the gray light, their words still clinging to him, and made his way to his car.

The wind off the coast cut through Liam's jacket as he neared the lighthouse. The cliffs rose beside him, and below, the ocean hammered the rocks.

The lighthouse stood above, blind and salt-stained, its beacon long extinguished. He stepped toward the base, realizing the world had gone still except for the sea.

Then it came. A bicycle bell. Faint. Out of place. The kind of sound that should have carried laughter behind it, but didn't.

Liam turned, breath slowing. Nothing moved. He scanned the trees, the path, and the brush near the lighthouse steps.

That's when he saw it. A cigarette, still burning. Smoke rising in a single thread. The filter was smeared with a thin line of red paint. The paper was hand-rolled. Familiar in a way he couldn't shake.

He crouched slowly. It hadn't been left by accident.

He scanned the ground. A single boot tread marked the dirt nearby, faint and shallow. There was no second step; it was just an impression. Like someone had paused, then vanished.

His pulse quickened. The sound, the cigarette, and the tread. They didn't add up, but they didn't have to. Whoever left them wasn't trying to hide.

He stood and turned toward the cliffs one last time. The sea raged on, indifferent. The lighthouse offered little. Only the feeling that something had been watching all along.

Back in town, the light had thinned. The windows at Millie's glowed. Inside, locals sat quietly, their gaze following as he passed. One nodded. One didn't.

A group of kids spilled out of Grayson's, their laughter high and sharp. But when they saw Liam, they stopped talking and watched. Not curious, expectant. Like they were waiting for something to begin.

He kept walking, as the story shifted. He felt it in his chest. This wasn't reporting anymore. It was an invitation. And he'd already accepted.

3

Whispers in the Mist

The fluorescent lights buzzed softly as Claire leaned against her cluttered desk at the Havenport Police Department. Across the room, the wall of case photos stared back at her: Victor Romero, Elliot Harris, Megan Sharpe, and Derek Marshall. Below each face, a small, twisted spoke gleamed under the cheap lighting.

Ben stood beside her, arms crossed, jaw tight. "It's getting harder to write these off as isolated events," he said, voice low. Four cyclists. Four broken spokes. Four weeks. That's not a coincidence."

"I know. This isn't random, it's deliberate."

Ben pulled out a chair and sat down. "And that's what makes it worse. This person isn't out of control. They're methodical."

Claire finally turned to him. "I don't think it's that simple. A broken spoke is minor to most people, but in cycling, it's the beginning of collapse. One piece fails; the whole thing can go."

Ben scoffed. "Sounds like symbolism to me. But not the poetic kind. They're throwing it in our faces."

"Or trying to throw the community off balance," Claire countered. "This isn't just about the victims. It's about the system they helped build."

Ben's frown deepened. "You're giving this person too much credit. They're not dismantling some metaphorical structure, Claire. They're killing people. One by one."

"And what if that's the point? To make us fixate on individuals and overlook the deeper break beneath it all?"

He looked back at the board, then down to the floor.

"She was supposed to ride with Derek last Saturday," Ben said. "My niece. He told her to skip it. Said the roads didn't feel right. She thought he was being overprotective. Now he's gone."

Claire didn't say anything. She didn't need to. Her posture had already shifted.

Claire finally spoke, her voice low but steady. "I know. And that's why I trust you with this. You're not just looking to solve a case. You're looking to protect what's still left to lose."

Ben let out a slow breath, his shoulders barely shifting. "That's the part that scares me the most," he said quietly. "Because if we're too late... I don't know how I would explain that."

Claire shifted. "I keep coming back to the why. That's how we get ahead of this. These attacks are not random. Someone's planning them, down to the smallest detail. That means there's logic inside the madness."

Ben didn't respond right away. He just studied her. "You sound like you're trying to make sense of it."

"I'm trying to get ahead of it," she said. "If we can understand the pattern, we have a shot at stopping it before another wheel snaps."

His jaw flexed. "Understanding a killer doesn't stop them."

"No," she admitted, softer now. "But it might give us a way in. Before your niece, or someone else, gets hurt."

Ben stood, letting her words hang between them. He looked again at the board. Then, with a hard edge to his voice, he said, "Let's talk about Ryan."

Claire stiffened. "What about him?"

"He's always there. First on the scene, asking questions. That's not just instinct. That's preparation."

"I've noticed," she said, carefully. "But being there doesn't make him guilty."

Ben didn't back off. "You're hesitating."

She didn't deny it. "Because it's complicated. He knows the scene, the people, the routes."

"Exactly," Ben said. "And that puts him in the center of the storm. You keep circling Ryan, Claire. If you're not questioning him, I will."

"I am questioning him. Every move he makes."

Ben tilted his head. "Then why does it seem like you're holding back?"

She looked away. "Because it's not that simple. He shows up because he's connected to the victims, to the roads, to all of it."

Ben's voice dropped. "And maybe to the killer."

Claire didn't respond right away. Her fingers tapped against the edge of the desk. "I don't know what to think," she admitted. "But I do know he's not just a name on a list."

Ben studied her. "You trust him."

"I don't know if I do," she said. "That's the problem."

"You've got instincts, Claire. But you're human. If there's something personal, interest, trust, curiosity, it can throw you off."

"This is about the case. Nothing else. I'm staying grounded in the facts."

Ben grabbed his notebook and turned toward the door. "Then let's keep it that way. I'll take Derek's last ride. Route, stops, conversations. Someone out there knows more than they're saying."

Claire gave a short nod. "Good. We catch the fracture before the whole wheel gives."

At the door, Ben stopped and glanced back. "If I'm wrong about Ryan, I'll own it. But if you are..."
  He didn't finish the sentence.

Claire turned back to the board. The victims' faces stared back, but her thoughts were somewhere else. If she was wrong about him, then the next break wasn't just coming, it was already in motion.

The front door opened with a sharp gust of wind, scattering loose paper across the front desk. Liam Harper stepped inside. He didn't pause or acknowledge the glances from the officers nearby.

She looked up from the board of case photos. "This better be good, Harper."

Liam didn't waste time. "It's about Ryan. I've been hearing things. Off-the-record stuff, but enough to matter. I think he could be the next target. Or worse."

Claire stepped away from the board, his words making her stomach turn. "Worse?"

He lowered his voice. "Some of the younger riders said Derek was acting strange before he died. A few think he was trying to warn Ryan."

"If that's true, why wouldn't Ryan come forward?"

Liam hesitated. "That's the part I can't figure out. Either Ryan didn't take it seriously, or he knows more than he's letting on."

Claire folded her arms. "You think he's involved?"

"I do," Liam said carefully. "Maybe not the killer, but he seems to be circling the dark truths. He's asking questions that make people nervous. Some won't talk to him at all. Others say he's digging too much."

Claire turned back to the board. Ryan's name wasn't on it, but it hovered in the air.

"If he's chasing the killer, he should be working with us," she said. "If he's not... we need to know why."

Liam studied her. "You're not convinced he's innocent."

"I'm not convinced of anything anymore," she replied. "But I do think he's connected. And if he's the next target, we're already behind."

"And if he's not a target?" Liam asked. "If he's the one we should be looking at?"

Claire didn't flinch. "Then we follow the evidence."

As Liam walked away, Claire stayed, tracing the pattern on the board. Four markers that wouldn't settle. And in the middle, one name that refused to fade: Ryan Moore.

Claire slipped on her coat; the moment had settled over her. Outside, the cold air met her face. The streets were empty as she made her way along the uneven sidewalks. She hurried, heading straight for the community center.

She pushed open the glass doors, met by a rush of warmth and the chaotic noise of kids shouting and basketballs hitting the floor. She looked toward Charlie Weston. The center coordinator was chatting with a group of volunteers by the front desk.

She headed straight for him, her words cutting through the room's hum. "Charlie."

Charlie turned, his expression shifting to surprise and concern. "Detective Sandoval," he greeted. "What's going on?"

"Have you seen Ryan Moore today?" Claire asked.

Charlie's face grew serious. "He was here earlier."

Her expression narrowed. "What was he doing?"

Charlie hesitated, then glanced around. "He was asking about Derek Marshall. Seemed pretty worked up."

She spotted Ben near the entrance, his face as rigid as hers. He approached, "No sign of him at the house. Is he here?"

Claire took a quick look around, then turned to Ben. "No, but someone might know where he went."

Ben nodded as he watched the bustling activity.

She leaned closer to Charlie. "Worked up how?"

"Like he was trying to make sense of it all," Charlie replied. "He kept asking if Derek had mentioned anything strange before he died. He was especially interested in the lighthouse."

A rush surged through her. "The lighthouse?"

"Yeah," Charlie confirmed. "Ryan kept asking if Derek had said anything about seeing lights out there. Or hearing voices."

Ben's expression darkened. "You think he's trying to retrace Derek's steps?"

Claire nodded. "It makes sense. Derek may have found something out there, and Ryan's trying to follow the same trail."

Charlie appeared worried. "If that's true, Ryan's putting himself in real danger. Derek came back from one of his last rides looking more shaken than usual. Said he saw lights near the cliffs where there shouldn't be any."

She exchanged a glance with Ben. "If Ryan's trying to find answers, he's going straight into the heart of this."

Ben's tone was urgent. "If he's anywhere near that lighthouse, we need to get there now."

Claire turned to Charlie, who was once again busying himself. "If Ryan shows up again, call me immediately. No matter what."

"Will do," Charlie promised, concern clear. "Be careful. Whatever's out there, it's not about the road anymore."

Claire nodded sharply, then turned to Ben. "Let's go."

As they rushed to the car, her mind was racing. If Ryan was close, they needed to be closer.

The drive was calm, although the air was full of anticipation. As they pulled onto the winding road, the buildings faded behind them. The lighthouse came into view, and they pulled up near the cliff's edge.

Claire turned off the engine.

Ben didn't move. "You think Ryan would come out here?"

"I don't know," she said. "But this place keeps showing up.

Photos, old stories, and people feeling things they shouldn't."

He looked at her sideways. "We've got no hard tie to this site. No witness, no prints, not even a sketchy receipt. Are you sure we're not chasing fog?"

Claire stared ahead. "That's the job. We chase the fog until it clears."

Ben gave a short shake of his head. "You used to hate that kind of talk. Said you didn't have the luxury of guesses."

"I still don't," she said, stepping out of the car. "But I'm learning to trust when something won't leave me alone."

The wind met them fast and sharp. Salt, wet stone, and the smell of cold air wrapped in secrets. They moved together across the gravel, the lighthouse getting closer with each step.

Claire walked along the side of the building. "The town barely funds upkeep. No regular maintenance. No tours in the off-season. If someone needed privacy, this is where they'd come."

Ben frowned. "It's too open. Too exposed."

"Which makes it perfect. Nobody expects anyone to be stupid enough to use it."

Ben sighed and followed. "You've got a special way of justifying crazy."

Claire didn't respond. She was already moving toward a narrow path behind the lighthouse that dropped toward the rocks. The ground was slick with moss and rain.

Halfway down the path, something fluttered in the brush, caught in a cluster of low vines. Claire paused and crouched beside it.

A torn edge of plastic peeked out; laminated, weather-stained, but intact enough to show a cluster of elevation lines and familiar markers.

Claire pulled it free and turned it over. "It's a cycling map."

Ben leaned in. "Harbor Loop. Last year's design. That's not an official marker, though."

She pointed to a crude X drawn in blue ink, right on the fringe of the map. It landed just outside the race route, right where they were standing.

Claire reached into her coat and pulled out a small field pouch, sliding the fragment into a clean plastic evidence sleeve. She sealed it and labeled the corner quickly.

"Too damp for prints, maybe, but if someone left this, they meant for it to be found. Or to send a message."

Ben straightened. "Could've been a random drop."

"Or it was planted. Or forgotten. Either way, it's something."

They stood there a moment longer, looking down at the map, then back up at the lighthouse.

Ben's voice was hushed now. "You've changed, you know."

Claire looked at him. "Is that good or bad?"

"It's... different. The Claire I met three years ago would've called this a waste of time."

Claire tucked the evidence bag into her pocket. "And the Ben I met three years ago would've driven off already."

He let out a short laugh. "Still might, if we keep chasing feelings."

She smiled faintly. "It's not just a feeling. It's a thread."

As they made their way back to the car, the wind picked up again, pushing against their backs. Claire glanced once more at the lighthouse.

"We're close," she said.

Ben opened the passenger door but didn't get in right away. "Close to what?"

"To understanding why this all started."

Ben looked out toward the cliffs. "What do we need to do to end this, once and for all?"

Claire didn't answer. She slid into the driver's seat with the evidence bag between them. As the engine rumbled to life, her mind was already racing, back to Ryan, to the whispers in town, to the unease building in her chest.

Far behind them, beyond the cliffs and the twisted trail from the lighthouse, the woods held their breath. Deep in the trees, silence ruled.

A sharp breath cut through the cold. Satisfaction flickered, edged with doubt. Every move carried purpose, every choice a piece of something larger.

Victor Romero's life ended where it needed to. He mistook order for control and structure for power. But power without limits always cracks. The broken spoke was not a calling card; it was truth laid bare. They believed he was the beginning, the one they built themselves around. When the frame cracks, everything collapses. He had to fall.

Elliot Harris moved like rules were for other people. Reckless. Charming enough to make everyone forget how often he crossed the line. That hill knew better. It keeps secrets. His death wasn't grief; it was stillness. Justice.

Megan Sharpe. Everyone's light, the peacemaker, the planner. But light blinds. She made them feel safe while others were invisible. Her end, on the edge of the forest where light dies, forced them to see what they had ignored all along.

Derek Marshall was the dependable one. Unshakable. Their

rock. Rocks are dangerous on fault lines. He kept them grounded in their lies, silencing the wrong voices to keep the peace. At the cliffs, the sea unsettled him. For once, the wind told the truth. His death wasn't chaos. It was a correction.

A slow breath from grim satisfaction. Havenport is unraveling. The real horrors are only beginning to wake.

Fingers closed around the rusted spoke, its jagged edges biting skin. It wasn't just a tool. It was a reminder of the gates that never opened. This isn't revenge, it's sorrow turned to purpose. The cyclists were only sparks. The real fire is meant to burn deeper.

There is logic in it. Cold, perfect logic. This was never about individuals, but about the world they represent, a culture that crowns its chosen few and discards the rest. Every strike is a message. Not written in ink but in blood. A declaration that no one is untouchable.

The next target is already marked. A new face, the same arrogance. A predictable routine. The hint of fatigue, the bend in the road where awareness blurs. This dark dance had refined itself.

Jacob Whitley would be out there, his neon jacket cutting through the night like a glowing symbol of misplaced confidence.

The stage was set; the moment had come. The wheel would turn again.

Unaware that someone was watching, Jacob mounted his bike, tightened his helmet and straps, and rode into the night. His measured movements cut through the stillness.

There was no thrill in this, only purpose. It wasn't personal; it was balanced. This wasn't about speed or violence. It was about control and the deliberate act of breaking things.

His neon figure moved through the night, his cadence smooth and unbroken. The feeling was familiar. The presence knew him well; his routines, his habits, his need to ride alone. That solitude made him easy to follow, easy to understand.

There was no rush; timing was everything. The game was still unfolding, and Jacob was another piece on the board, part of something much older than any of them realized.

The broken spoke wasn't meant to take him. Not yet. It was a reminder, a warning to Jacob, and to all of them. The road was no longer safe. Nothing in the cycling world could be trusted; not the routes, the riders, or even those they thought they knew best.

As he rounded a sharp bend and disappeared, a suffocating stillness took hold; a fitting cover for the darkness that gripped the streets and the lives within them.

There was no rush, just a slow burn of anticipation. The familiar burn had already gripped his legs, a satisfying strain of muscle against resistance. For him, cycling was more than a habit. It was a nightly purge of frustration and fear. The one place where his thoughts could finally let go.

The road was slick with drizzle, the asphalt glowing beneath the beam of his headlamp. The sound of the tires cutting through small puddles was comforting, a reminder that the bike beneath him was dependable and strong.

Each turn of the pedals was calming. He wasn't a racer, driven by the hunger for speed or competition. He was riding for the love of it, finding a freedom that had always eluded him.

His mind wandered as he rode, his thoughts drifting to the recent deaths that had shaken the cycling network. He had known them all, each in different ways.

Each night, he rode with a growing sense of nervousness. It wasn't the darkness; it was the feeling of being watched. He told himself it was nerves. Yet deep down, his instincts screamed otherwise.

He glanced over his shoulder. Nothing. No headlights, no movement in the dark. No sign of the dark figure rumored to haunt these routes. It was him and the empty road.

Jacob shook off the paranoia, leaning forward into a more aerodynamic position as the road inclined. His legs burned pleasantly. He concentrated on breathing, inhaling through his nose, and exhaling through his mouth. Controlling his pace, he told himself he was safe. These roads were his sanctuary.

His mind wandered. Work, family, and the upcoming charity ride that Megan had been organizing before her death. A pang of guilt hit him at the thought of her. Wishing he'd done more to help her, that he'd been there more. Protect her somehow.

He had always admired her resilience, her kindness, and her ability to see the good in people. It was cruel, he thought, that someone like her could be taken in such a brutal way.

The road sloped downward, signaling the end of his ride. He relaxed his grip, letting the bike gain speed. A quick thrill shot through him as he coasted, the wind slicing through his jacket and filling him with a weightless joy. For an instant, he was free, like he could outrun the darkness.

He reached the bottom of the hill and rolled to a stop, breathing heavily, feeling satisfied. Ahead was his small cottage, a welcome sight. He dismounted, legs a bit shaky, and wheeled the bike up to the porch. The ride had drained him more than usual, but oddly, relief washed over him.

Jacob leaned the bike against the railing. A shiver ran down his spine as he became aware of his isolation. He shook it off, telling himself it was the cold seeping through his clothes.

Inside, the cottage was warm and softly lit. He switched on a few more lights, trying to push away the darkness that followed him inside. He shrugged off his neon jacket, draped it over a chair, and kicked off his shoes. On the way to the bathroom, he peeled off his sweat-soaked clothes.

Stepping into the shower, he turned the water as hot as he could stand. Steam filled the small space as he relaxed, letting the heat ease his tired muscles. The water washed away the sweat, the grime, and some of the remaining strain.

As the water ran over him, exhaustion sank into his bones. He finished his shower, stepped into the steamy bathroom, and wiped the mirror. He looked at his reflection; tired eyes and a worn face stared back at him. A man who'd survived another ride, knowing the danger wasn't over.

Later, still restless, Jacob sat at his desk and opened his laptop. The screen glowed pale in the dim room. He clicked into a blank email and typed slowly, not intending to send it, just needing the words to exist somewhere.

I don't know what's happening anymore. Every time I hear a siren, I freeze. I know I wasn't as close with them as some, but they were part of this world. Our world. And now they're gone.

At first, I thought it was just bad luck. But I've ridden these roads long enough to know the difference between random and deliberate. Something's out there. Watching. Waiting. No one wants to say it, but we all feel it.

I tried to talk to Ryan but couldn't find the words. What am I supposed to say? That I'm scared? That I keep seeing things? That I've started skipping the old climbs because they feel... wrong?

I tell myself to keep my head down. Ride smart. Stay alert. But it's not helping. The group's quieter now. People are avoiding eye contact, changing routes, and canceling rides. We're pretending nothing's changed, but everything has.

He stared at the screen for a long moment, then closed the laptop.

Outside, the wind pressed against the windows, low and insistent. Jacob stood and moved to the couch, but dread followed him.

He left the lights on, just in case.

4

Veil of Deception

The scent of oil and rubber filled Marissa Lane's bike shop, mixing with the faint aroma of aged wood from the worn workbench. The small space was orderly yet cluttered. Tools were neatly hung on the walls. Their gleaming surfaces reflected her meticulous nature. Bicycles in various states of repair lined the room, each one a testament to her skill and precision.

The gears clicked softly under Marissa's touch, her movements smooth and unhurried, the work second nature by now. She carried a sharpness that hinted at old battles she never quite forgot. Something inside her had been clenched for so long that it had become part of her.

She glanced toward the window as a cyclist sped past. The flash of a neon caught her attention. Her hand paused for half a second as her jaw tightened. Cycling had been the pulse of her life, her breath, freedom, and fire. Now it was something she kept at a distance, just far enough to let her breathe without pain.

The front bell chimed. She didn't look up right away.

A boy entered, no older than ten. He hesitated at the threshold, taking in the shop with wide, unsure eyes.

"My mom said you could fix it," he pointed at the chain on the bike he had dragged in.

Marissa let the silence sit a moment longer than necessary, long enough for him to wonder if he'd made a mistake.

Then she stood, wiped her hands on a rag, and nodded toward the bike.

"Bring it over." She motioned for him to join her.

He did, carefully, like he wasn't sure how close he was allowed to get.

She crouched beside it, her fingers already finding the slack in the chain. Years of muscle memory guided her hands. She didn't look at him.

"You ride a lot?"

The boy nodded. "Every day. I'm practicing."

She checked the rear cassette, then turned the crank gently. "Practicing for what?"

He shrugged. "I dunno... to get better, I guess."

A pause.

"I like feeling fast."

Marissa didn't say anything at first, but something flicked in her chest. That word... *fast.* It used to mean something. It used to mean everything.

She tightened the chain, adjusted the derailleur, and tested the gears with quick, precise movements. The work grounded her. She'd always trusted her hands more than her words.

"There," she said. "It'll hold for now. Tell your mom it'll need a full tune-up soon."

The boy looked down at the bike with admiration, as if she'd just fixed something far more important than a chain.

"Were you a racer or something?" he asked. "My uncle said you used to win all the time."

Marissa's body stiffened as she ran a finger along the crank arm. "I used to ride."

"That's cool," he said. "You probably still could. You look like someone who still could."

He said it without meaning. No expectations. Just a fact, like he was stating the weather. But it landed hard.

The boy started toward the door, then turned back with a shy smile. "Thanks."

The bell chimed again as he left, the sound soft but lingering.

Marissa stood in place for a long time; her fingers still curled around the wrench. Her mind was somewhere else. Somewhere older.

She walked back to the bench, sat down, and stared at the tools laid out before her. Everything was in its place, how she liked it.

But her hands didn't move. Not right away.

She didn't know what startled her more: that a kid had seen something in her she thought was gone, or that for a moment, she wanted to believe him.

The bell rang above the door once again. Marissa looked up, her face shifting. Liam Harper stepped inside, casual as always.

"Morning, Marissa," he said, voice probing. "Figured I'd find you here."

She raised an eyebrow, her tone cool. "Where else would I be?"

"I was hoping to talk to you about what's been happening. People are rattled, and I'm piecing together a story."

Marissa's expression didn't change. "I fix bikes, Liam. That's all I do now."

"Not true." He leaned on the counter, studying her. "You were part of this world. You know these roads better than anyone, the rivalries, the risks."

Her fingers tightened on the wrench. "That was a lifetime ago."

"Not for the people who remember. You were legendary," Liam pressed. "With these murders, your name keeps coming up. People think you might see something the rest of us can't."

She looked up, guarded. "What I see is tragedy. And I've stayed out of that world for a reason."

"You expect me to believe you don't have thoughts on this?" His voice sharpened. "You knew these riders. Maybe even rode with them."

Marissa's jaw tightened. "Everything changed," she said. "That's why I keep my distance."

Liam leaned closer. "You can't stay on the sidelines forever. I know there is a part of you that still cares."

She faced him. "Maybe you're right," she admitted. "But I'm not talking."

"Why not?" he challenged. "People trust you. If anyone can bring sense to this, it's you. I'm not asking for secrets, just perspective. Before more people get hurt."

Her lips curved into a faint, humorless smile. "Maybe some things are better left unsaid."

Liam tilted his head, unrelenting. "Who are you protecting, Marissa? Yourself, or someone else?"

The question landed like a blow. "You've got some nerve, Liam. Be careful what you dig for. The truth isn't always something you want to find."

He studied her, his tone softening. "Ugly truths don't scare me. They make me look harder."

Marissa didn't blink. "Then make sure you know where you're digging."

"I do," Liam said. "And I think you do too."

Silence. Liam finally stepped back, sensing the line he had pushed.

"Think about it," he said, focusing on her. "I'm not done with this story, or with you."

Marissa watched him head for the door. "Be careful, Liam," she called after him. "This town isn't as simple as it looks."

He paused at the threshold, a wry smile flickering. "Neither are you."

Marissa froze in place, her mind spinning. She glanced down at the workbench, her fingers absently brushing against a broken spoke lying among her tools. She picked it up, feeling its heft in her hand, its sharp edges digging into her palm.

She turned to the window, tracing the familiar outlines. The streets, usually buzzing with life, were hushed. Liam's figure held in the distance, gradually fading into the mist.

Marissa's thoughts turned darker. Was she shielding herself, as Liam suggested, or was she part of a larger, more dangerous game?

Outside, the day moved on. The mourners had gathered. Their dark coats blended with the muted colors of early Fall. A cool, crisp breeze filled the hillside cemetery. A hint of wood smoke and sea salt carried through the breeze. The sky was overcast. Casting a soft gray light over the faded reds and golds of the autumn leaves.

Megan Sharpe's funeral was underway, and the small crowd huddled close by. Grief hung in the air, binding them in quiet sorrow. This wasn't just another funeral. It was a stark reminder of the mystery that persisted.

Near the front of the gathering, Megan's parents stood together. Her mother, Marianne, clutched a single white rose to her chest, her gloved hands trembling. She stared blankly ahead, trying to make sense of a world without her daughter.

Thomas Sharpe stood rigid at her side, his hand firmly over

hers. His jaw was set, but the tears streaking down his weathered face exposed the ache he could no longer contain. Every so often, his eyes drifted toward the casket, his expression darkening with grief.

Claire watched them from a distance. She had attended many funerals in her time, but this one felt different. Heavier, closer, and sharper. The kind of pain that leaves a mark.

As she scanned the area, she spotted Ryan standing near the edge. His back was turned; shoulders hunched against the cold. He wore dark jeans, a wool jacket, and a black beanie pulled low over his messy hair. He seemed worn out, older somehow. Megan had been one of his closest friends. Seeing him here made everything more complicated.

Ben nudged Claire. "You gonna talk to him?"

She shook her head. "Not now," she replied. "It's not the right time. Let him grieve."

She couldn't shake the growing need to talk with Ryan, to get to the truth. Hesitation kept her there. Maybe it was the rawness or the genuine look of loss on his face. Confronting him here, surrounded by mourners and memories, wouldn't lead anywhere.

Behind her, two older men stood near the stone wall, speaking just above a whisper.

"Strange how they all passed the quarry that day," one of them said. "You'd think with everything going on, they'd stick to safer ground."

The words weren't meant for her, yet they landed like a soft tap against her mind. It wasn't a lead. It wasn't even new. But something about it lodged itself there.

Claire didn't write it down. She didn't analyze it; she felt it. For once, she didn't push it aside.

She had spent most of her career demanding evidence before following a hunch. But now, something had shifted.

Maybe it was the pattern of the deaths or the way her breath caught every time someone mentioned the fog, the roads, or the quiet. Maybe it was just that her instincts had earned their place.

She stood a little straighter, looking past Ryan to the ridgeline beyond the cemetery.

Hidden beneath the shade of an old pine, Liam stood just out of sight. His posture looked casual, but sharp. He pulled out his notepad, its pages worn from constant use, and began to write with quick, deliberate strokes.

He wasn't simply recording facts. Liam dissected the scene, pulling it apart piece by piece. Years of reporting had taught him distance, but as he watched the mourners around Megan's casket, that thin veil of professionalism felt frayed. There was an edge in his notes, a personal tone, as if every line was a way to wrestle with his own unease.

Megan's funeral was more than a service. It was a wound laid bare. Her absence had carved something out of Havenport, leaving a hole that felt larger than the town itself. The sorrow stretched far beyond the cycling community.

He paused, glancing toward Ryan. Standing at the edge of the crowd, Ryan stood apart from the rest, shoulders hunched, head lowered, as though he was carrying more.

Liam's pen hesitated over the page before writing: *Grief can hide guilt as easily as sorrow.*

Then he shifted towards Claire. She stood slightly back, looking at Megan's parents. There was stiffness in her stance that Liam recognized, something pulling her in two directions.

He knew that look. He had worn it himself when he was too close to a story to see it. He considered walking over and testing her reaction. Instead, he stayed still. Claire's unease was telling enough.

His pen moved again. *This isn't just a murder story. It's a reckoning.*

The crowd began to thin, footsteps crunching over fallen leaves. Liam closed his notepad. Ryan didn't move, and neither did Claire. There was something unspoken between them, something Liam couldn't name, but he felt it.

He paused for a moment, the wind snapping against his jacket. This story wasn't just cold. It was alive. And whatever haunted this town was far from finished.

Claire and Ben remained, watching Ryan as he bowed his head in somber reflection.

As they turned to leave, a soft voice called out behind them. "Detective."

Claire turned to find Marianne standing there, her hand clutching the now-wilted rose. Thomas was at her side, his expression unreadable, though it spoke volumes. There was a hollowness in Marianne, but beneath it burned a desperate determination.

"Please," Marianne asked. "Find who did this to our daughter."

Thomas gave a slow nod. "Promise us you'll bring them to justice."

"We will," she vowed. "I promise."

Ben stood beside her. "We won't stop until we do."

Claire stepped forward, her voice low but steady. "I'm sorry for your loss. Truly."

Ben gave a small nod beside her. "We both are."

Marianne's lips trembled, but she managed to nod in thanks. Thomas gently guided her away, his arm around her shoulders. Together, they walked to the waiting car, leaving Claire and Ben standing together, their promise pressing between them.

"Are you sure we should wait?" Ben asked, pulling his coat tighter.

Claire nodded, though uncertainty flashed on her face. "We will. But not for long." She glanced at Ryan, her expression unreadable. "Whatever he knows, we need to find out soon."

Ben sighed, glancing at Liam's distant figure. "He's already written half the story, hasn't he?"

"Maybe," She replied. "It's the other half I'm worried about."

With that, they turned to leave the cemetery. For now, the one certainty was that Megan's death was just one shadow in a larger darkness, and the rest had yet to surface.

By afternoon, the cycling community had gathered at Millie's Diner, filling the cozy space with warmth and a low hum of conversation.

In one corner, Tommy leaned over the table, voice dropping.

"I swear, it was like he was hunting us," he said. "This rider... all black bike, no lights, no markings. Fastest thing I've ever seen. It wasn't that he passed you. He made you feel like you didn't belong."

A few in the group shifted uneasily.

Lena quietly asked, "Where do people see him?"

Tommy's mouth curved in a nervous grin. "They say up on the old coastal road, near the lighthouse. Some think he's a warning, others say he's a reminder."

A hush crept over the table. Ryan stood slightly apart, hands shoved into his pockets. His expression was guarded.

Tommy caught the look and smirked. "Come on, Ryan. You and Megan rode that stretch more than anyone. Don't tell me you never felt something off out there."

Ryan looked at Tommy. "People like ghost stories," he said, voice flat. "Doesn't make them real."

Lena's brow furrowed. "A rider who shows up and disappears without a trace. That's not just a story."

Ryan gave a small shrug. "Could be someone who wants the road to himself. Not everything is a mystery."

Sarah tilted her head, studying him. "You rode with Megan all the time. You never saw anything strange?"

His jaw tightened. "I'm not saying nothing's out there," he said after a pause. "I just think Megan would want us working on something real. On watching out for each other. Not chasing ghosts."

Tommy started to press again, but Jasper gave a subtle shake of his head, warning him to let it go. Ryan turned back to the window, his shoulders stiff.

Then Max spoke, hesitating before the words came out. "If someone's behind this... what about Marissa? She's kept her distance, but she knows these roads better than anyone. After her crash, she just... changed. Cold. Like she's still watching all of us."

A ripple went through the group. Sarah frowned, considering it. "She does know how we all ride. Every route, every weakness. If anyone could plan something like this..."

Lena didn't speak, but her silence said enough.

Ryan turned, his voice cutting through the quiet. "No. Marissa isn't part of this."

Tommy raised an eyebrow. "You sound sure."

"She lost everything out there," Ryan said firmly. "The accident, the racing. She's not plotting revenge. She's trying to survive."

Max muttered, "Or hiding in plain sight."

Ryan's glare shut him down.

The group shifted, speaking instead about Megan; her grit, her humor, the rides they had shared. But the ghost rider hovered like an unwelcome thought.

Millie approached with a fresh pot of coffee, listening as she poured. "I've heard my share of stories about that road," she said. "The fog there hides more than the past."

A hush followed her words. Everyone knew that stretch of coastal road, with its winding cliffs, jagged drop-offs, and the kind of stillness that unnerves even seasoned riders.

Jasper spoke with a thoughtful calm. "Megan used to say that road had a spirit of its own. She rode it like she was trying to understand it; like she sensed something the rest of us couldn't see."

No one replied.

Lena's attention returned to Tommy. "Do you think this rider's connected to her?"

Tommy shook his head. "I don't know. But every time I think about it, I can't shake the feeling he's out there."

His words lingered after the conversation faded, hanging in the warm air like the steam rising from forgotten mugs. One by one, the riders drifted out into the dim evening, the diner door chiming softly behind them.

Outside, Havenport lay wrapped in a creeping fog. The streets were quiet, washed in the dull orange glow of tired streetlamps. Tires hissed faintly somewhere far off, then were gone.

Ryan stepped out last, pausing on the sidewalk as the door swung shut behind him. Through the glass, the empty tables sat in stillness, holding the echoes of the voices that had filled them.

Marissa's name still clung to the air. Not with grief this time, but with doubt.

He shoved his hands into his jacket pockets and stared down the deserted street, its winding stretch disappearing into gray. They were all looking for someone to blame, and tonight, their fear had found her.

But fear has a way of warping truth, and of missing what waits in the shadows.

Ryan turned and walked into the mist, the town settling behind him. The roads were waiting, and whatever haunted them wasn't done.

II

The Hunt Begins

5

The Dark Descent

Marissa sat alone in her small cottage, staring at the gloom beyond the window. A thin draft slipped through a crack she had left open; a chill she welcomed for its honesty.

She cupped a mug of black tea, the heat pressing into her skin. Chamomile was for gentler nights. Black tea suited her now, bitter enough to cut through the memories.

The accident had been sudden and brutal. One moment, she was flying, in control. Then the slick patch, the wrong angle, the sound of metal folding in on itself, and the ground rushing up.

She had fought to recover, inch by inch, but she was not built for patience. She was built for speed, for the pulse of danger. Rehab demanded humility and stillness, a body forced to start over.

The physical pain was manageable. It was the loneliness that carved deepest. She had not just lost her strength; she had lost her place. The early rides, the camaraderie, the laughter after a brutal climb. That world had shaped her.

Her mind shifted to the old bike in the corner, its frame dulled by dust. She could ride again, but not the way she used to. Not with the fire that once made her feel alive.

Megan was new when Marissa was a name people cheered for. They were never close, but Marissa recognized her spirit; she burned with a constant fire. The kind that doesn't wait for permission. Marissa sometimes wanted to warn her how fast the highs could turn, but she never did. Now she was gone.

The room cooled as the light faded. She pulled her sweater tight, the scratch of the wool grounding her. The tea had gone cold, but she held the mug anyway. She set it down, harder than she intended, and moved to the window. Outside, stars pierced the night sky.

The wind shifted. Somewhere beyond the trees came the sound of laughter. Riders finishing a late session. That sound used to be hers. A pulse of longing hit her, quick and uninvited. Then came the resentment.

She was too tired to keep fighting for a place in it.

As dusk settled over Havenport, life continued at its uneasy pace. The sky deepened as Jacob pushed open the door to The Haven Café. The warmth met him instantly. Inside, the mingled scents of coffee and cider softened the sharp bite of the evening air.

The café was quieter than usual. The usual cluster of cyclists sat close together, their faces drawn in the flickering light. Beneath the surface chatter, anxiety pulled like static.

"Jacob! Over here!" Tommy called.

He made his way over. "Evening," Jacob greeted, his voice low. "Figured you'd all be here."

"Can't let a little darkness keep us away," Kayla said, managing a thin smile. She handed him a cup of coffee. "Or a lot of darkness."

Jacob took the mug, wrapping his fingers in the warmth. "Feels like we need this more than ever."

Tommy leaned in. "Especially after Derek. It's like the streets aren't ours anymore."

Kayla stared into her cup. "It's the spoke. Always the broken spoke." Her voice faltered. "Same as the others. Just lying there."

Jacob felt the chill crawl down his spine. "It's a message. Someone wants us to unravel."

He didn't raise his voice, but there was steel in it. "That's exactly why we ride. To push back. To stay present."

Nate looked up. "It has changed. I used to love night rides. Now it feels like something's watching."

"That fear only grows if we allow it to." Jacob declared.

Tommy's usual bravado had dimmed. "What if the Ghost Rider is real? What if someone's out there waiting?"

Jacob's jaw tensed. "Then we ride smarter. Stay sharp. But we keep riding. The road doesn't belong to fear."

Kayla's voice trembled. "What if it's one of us next?"

Jacob reached across the table, resting a hand on her arm. His touch was firm, grounding. "Then we stand together. We ride like we always have. No one gets left behind."

The others nodded, but the unease didn't lift. Their talk shifted to race prep and gear upgrades. The laughter that followed was brief and hollow; more habit than joy.

Jacob stood, draining the last of his coffee. "Alright. I'm heading out. Thought I'd take the long loop. Clear my head before the weekend."

"You're going now?" Tommy asked, worry breaking through. "Alone?"

Jacob nodded. "Yeah. Darkness isn't going anywhere. Neither am I."

Kayla gave a soft sigh. "Just... be careful."

His smile came easily. "Always careful, Kayla. But I've got to ride."

He stepped outside, and the cold hit him like a wave. The street was still. No wind, no voices. Only the distant sound of waves breaking beyond the trees.

Jacob mounted his bike. The frame felt solid beneath him, his legs falling into motion as he pushed into the night. The streetlights faded behind him, swallowed by the gloom, the wet pavement catching what little light remained.

The road curved past the old quarry, its chain-link fence sagging with rust. The black water below shimmered faintly, still as glass. Jacob slowed, scanning the fence line. A faint crunch of gravel made his pulse quicken. He waited, breath tight, but saw nothing. With a burst of effort, he rose from the seat and pedaled hard until the quarry vanished from view.

Then he heard it. Tires on wet pavement. Not his. Behind him. He twisted around. Nothing.

His heart thudded, sharp and hollow, and for a moment he almost turned back toward the glow of town. Instead, he lowered his head and pushed forward, settling into the rhythm that had always calmed him. Smooth circles. Even breath. Keep going.

Jacob had never been the fastest or the most relentless. He had just... stayed. Survived every crash, every storm, every slow unraveling of people he'd once thought unbreakable.

Survivor. That was what people called him now, as if endurance alone made him whole. As if outlasting everyone else hadn't carved something out of him.

He remembered Megan's laugh echoing across the café, how it used to fill the gaps when silence grew too heavy. Derek's steady nod at the start of every ride, a silent promise that they'd all come back. Now they were names whispered in lowered voices, turned into cautionary tales and framed photos on memorial flyers.

He clenched the handlebars tighter. Part of him hated how quickly the group had fractured after their deaths. Routes changed, group rides canceled, quietly spreading like mold. Everyone pretended the roads were still safe. He had joined them in pretending. Maybe that made him worse.

The air grew colder as the road climbed toward the ridge. Trees crowded close on both sides, their dripping branches forming a tunnel that swallowed sound. His headlamp beam bounced across the pavement. Every shadow seemed to twitch.

There it was again; faint, steady, behind him. Tires whispering through puddles.

Jacob slowed, listening. The sound faded. He exhaled, shaky, and almost laughed at himself.

You're fine. Just nerves.

Still, he didn't look back again. He leaned into the hill, legs burning, lungs pulling deep, ragged air. The pain helped; pain meant real, meant alive.

Somewhere ahead, an owl called. The cry echoed through the trees, sharp and mournful.

Jacob thought of the email he'd half-written, words he hadn't been brave enough to send. *I don't think it's bad luck anymore. It feels like something is choosing us.* He'd closed the laptop before finishing it. Admitting it out loud would make it real.

His light caught on a reflective road sign up ahead, the sudden glare making him flinch. When his vision cleared, the road ahead was empty; too empty.

The quiet settled around him. The kind of quiet that waited.

A single drop of cold water struck the back of his neck. He jolted, glancing up. The branches above were still.

The sound came again, closer now. Jacob's chest tightened. He pressed harder, breath rough in his throat. "Who's there?"

No answer. Only the hiss of his tires and the pounding in his ears.

A shape appeared ahead, another rider.

The figure glided forward, movements smooth and unhurried, as if it had always been there. The black bike gleamed under the thin light, wheels whispering over the pavement.

Jacob's pulse surged. He stood on the pedals, muscles burning, trying to break away. The figure closed the gap with effortless speed.

"Stop!" he shouted, fear breaking through his voice.

The rider shifted suddenly, cutting across his front wheel.

Jacob's tire caught. The road tilted beneath him. He hit hard, ribs jolting from the impact. His bike skidded to the side, the frame screaming against the asphalt.

Pain shot through him, but he rolled, scrambling to push up. A gloved hand slammed into his chest, shoving him back down with surprising force.

"Get off me!" Jacob shouted, twisting. His boots scraped the wet pavement. He grabbed the figure's arm, trying to throw it off balance. The grip tightened.

A flash of metal; a broken spoke, jagged and rusted, raised high.

Jacob kicked hard, his heel catching the killer's leg. The spoke came down in a single strike, sinking into his side with brutal accuracy.

Jacob's breath tore from him in a strangled gasp. The gloved hand clamped over his mouth, pinning him to the road. He thrashed, but the strength drained out of him fast, cold creeping into his limbs.

A voice, low and measured, brushed his ear. "It was always going to be you."

The words sank into him like ice. Not rage or triumph. Just certainty.

Jacob's mind flashed through the café, the warm lights, the hollow smiles. The way people looked at him as proof that things were still normal. He had carried that weight quietly, pretending he couldn't feel it. Pretending survival was the same as safety.

Comfort makes them forget, the voice whispered, almost to itself. *Comfort keeps the machine alive.*

His vision dimmed.

The broken spoke was set beside him with unsettling care, like a marker on a grave. Then the pressure eased, and the figure slipped away into the trees; swift, silent, already gone.

A dense hush spread over the road. Blood and tire marks blurred, dissolving into the wet air. A single night bird called once. Then nothing.

In the trees, the killer paused.

Victor had ruled with control, convinced order could hold the chaos back. Elliot had raced on arrogance, daring the world to catch him. Megan had blinded them with light, and Derek had stilled them with rhythm.

But Jacob... Jacob had done something worse. He had made them believe they were safe.

Comfort is the strongest lie. Break that, and the whole wheel comes apart.

They turned from the road, the spoke's cold edge biting their palm. The quiet shuddered and then obeyed.

As dawn broke, the sky shifted from inky black to muted gray. Morning stretched out thin and pale, barely enough to cut through the fatigue in Claire's bones. Light crept across her kitchen, stretching over the table, now buried in notes, photos, and the clutter of a sleepless night.

The burden of the investigation refused to fade. The darkness hadn't left with the night; it had sunk into her chest. She had worked straight through, chasing facts, timelines, and correlations. But this morning, even the evidence felt exhausted. Hollow and incomplete.

Every corner of her apartment reflected the case now. A loose grid of newspaper clippings spread across the table. Each headline whispered the same thing: something is wrong. Each photo froze a moment in time. She stared at them. It wasn't just in the dates or distances. It was in the people. In the things left unsaid.

One clipping caught her attention again. Megan Sharpe. Smiling, open, and alive. Claire's note beside it read: *Community cornerstone. Why her?*

She picked it up and studied the image. It wasn't evidence anymore; it was a memory. Megan was someone people leaned on. Someone who held others together. For a moment, it felt like she was looking back at her. Not just with warmth, but with something else. A question, maybe, or a challenge. Asking her to see more than just the motive.

Claire leaned back in her chair. This was the part she never said out loud. That when logic ran dry, something remained. Intuition, maybe. She had trained herself to ignore it, to follow procedure. But lately, that wasn't enough.

She drifted to a faded memory. A night Megan had shown up at her door, late and unannounced. They had shared tea on the fire escape. She hadn't said much, her attention lost somewhere beyond the glass.

"They only trust me because I smile," she had said. "If I stopped, I don't think they'd follow."

Claire hadn't known what to say then. She still didn't. But she remembered the look on Megan's face; tired, like someone carrying too much and pretending it was light.

She reached for another article, this one from the Coastal Courier. *Havenport's Cycling Club – Thriving or Divided?* At first, it had seemed harmless. Now it reads differently. She underlined a paragraph about the growing conflict between veterans and newer riders.

In the margin, she wrote: *Personal or professional grudges involved?*

Even as she wrote it, she knew it wasn't enough. Too clean and easy. This wasn't about rivalry; it was about fractures. Secrets no one was ready to say out loud.

Claire didn't need more headlines. She needed to understand why these people had stopped trusting each other. And why were they all so afraid to name what was breaking?

Her phone buzzed on the table. Sergeant Ian Granger's name lit up the screen. She answered, already bracing.

"Claire, we've got another one. Jacob Whitley. Found near the old brewery. Off Route 7."

She stared at the note she'd written hours ago: *If assailant is pushing boundaries, what's the next escalation?*

Now she had her answer.

The call ended. Then a second buzz.

A text from Ben: *It's bad.*

Claire didn't move. Her hand hovered over the phone, fingers curled, as if it might burn her if she picked it up again. Her gaze drifted to the board on the far wall, to Megan's photo tacked in the center.

Something in it caught her; the angle of Megan's smile, the bright eyes that now belonged to someone dead.

Not the headline, or the pattern. The person.

A hollow ache bloomed in her chest, sharp and deep and terrifyingly familiar.

The overdose case surfaced, not as a memory but as a sensation. The smell of disinfectants, the rasp of the mother's breath, her trembling hands gripping Claire's wrists like they were the only thing left holding her upright.

You were supposed to see her.

Claire had buried that voice for years. She told herself grief made people irrational, and guilt wasn't evidence. She told herself she had done everything she could.

But tonight, the truth broke through like black water seeping through cracked stone. She hadn't missed the signs because they weren't there. She had missed them because she hadn't wanted to see them.

And maybe, just maybe, that's what she was doing now.

Chasing data points, timelines, neat cause-and-effects. Pretending the lines on the board meant something while her gut screamed that none of this was linear, that something darker was threading through the chaos, and she was too afraid to name it.

Her stomach twisted. Jacob had been the quiet one, the safe one, the reason the others still rode at all. If even he wasn't safe, then safety itself was the lie.

For the first time in days, her professional detachment cracked. Anger surged up through the hollow space grief had left behind; cold, bladed, and aimed squarely at herself.

If she let this keep happening, she wasn't a detective. She was a bystander with a badge.

Claire shoved her chair back so hard it skidded, grabbed her keys, and forced her body into motion before the weight could anchor her to the floor.

As she stepped into the night, she cast one last glance at the board: at the tangled lines, the names, the faces. The kitchen was silent except for the hum of the refrigerator, a small domestic noise that suddenly felt obscene, as if it belonged to a different life.

Outside, the air smelled like rain. The pavement was slick under her boots. The town was still pretending it could be safe, but she couldn't pretend anymore.

On the corner of Main Street, Millie's Diner was glowing. But inside, the hum of conversation had changed. The clink of cups and plates rang louder than usual, each sound cutting through the sorrow like glass.

Behind the counter, Millie moved with precision. Her hands filled mugs and slid plates across the counter without pause, but her usual warmth was dulled. The diner, once filled with easy laughter and morning chatter, had shifted into a space of low murmurs and glances that stayed a moment too long.

Pete, an old fisherman with a silver beard, leaned on the counter. His fingers curled loosely around his coffee, unmoving.

"Saw Jacob yesterday," he said, almost to himself. "Near the old brewery road. Seemed off." He paused. "Didn't think much of it then. Wish I'd stopped."

At a table nearby, Ellen sat with her daughter, clutching her mug so tightly her knuckles had gone white.

"My daughter doesn't want to go out after dark. The kids feel it, Millie. They're scared." Her voice wavered as she glanced toward the corner booth, where a small group of younger locals sat huddled together, speaking in whispers.

"You'd think," she continued, "in a town like this... we'd be safe."

Millie nodded without answering. She looked over at the group by the window, Jacob's friends. From the hollow looks on their faces, they already knew. Their conversation was low and clipped, carrying more helplessness than anger.

Even the dishes seemed subdued, each clink absorbed by the diner's uneasy hush. People leaned into their thoughts, into their fears, held together only by Millie's grounding presence.

She moved between tables, offering what reassurances she could. Her smile was soft. As she refilled Pete's cup, her voice dropped.

"A broken spoke," she said, barely audible. "Who does something like that?"

Frank sat with a few others at a back table. Their faces were usually full of banter and big plans. Not today. Frank set down his fork and looked around.

"Jacob wasn't just any rider. He was one of ours." His voice cracked. "And now..."

He trailed off, fixed on the coffee in front of him, as if it might hold the answers no one had.
    The diner fell silent again. A shared understanding filled the room.

Jacob's death was more than another loss. It was the moment safety slipped away.

No one said it aloud, but behind every hushed voice and shifting glance, the same question remained.

Who would be next?

6

Secrets in the Fog

The road where Jacob Whitley's body was found was quiet. The tall pines stood motionless, their branches dripping onto the wet pavement with soft, hollow taps. A faint metallic scent clung to the damp air.

Claire stood near the body, her face unreadable. Jacob's limbs were twisted unnaturally, a broken spoke beside him. The placement was precise, intimate. It turned her stomach, but she didn't let it show.

Nearby, officers moved carefully, voices low, blending with the crackle of radios. Claire glanced toward the turnoff near the quarry. *The quarry again. Why there? Why is it always close to it?*

The mist curled low across the pavement, swallowing the edges of the floodlights. Yellow tape sagged between metal stakes, slick with rain, flapping weakly in the breeze.

Claire ducked beneath it. The world inside the tape felt muted, muffled, as though sound itself was holding its breath. The smell of wet asphalt and chain oil lingered faintly, ghostlike.

She walked to the dark patch where Jacob's body had been, boots sinking slightly in the softened shoulder of the road. The bike was gone, but its absence seemed louder than its presence ever could have been.

She crouched, her gloved hand hovering above the damp gravel. Tire grooves glistened faintly under her flashlight, already smudged by the drizzle. A few stones had been scattered toward the ditch as though kicked in panic. A single chain link lay twisted in the gutter, rusted at the edges; she couldn't tell if it had broken tonight or years ago.

This was supposed to be Jacob's safe route. Predictable and familiar. That was why he had chosen it. That was why they had all quietly believed he would survive this.

Her gaze followed a faint disruption in the gravel leading toward the tree line. It bent, then vanished, swallowed by shadow.

A hollow pressure tightened behind her ribs. She had been waiting for a pattern to emerge; certain it would appear if she just stared hard enough. But maybe the pattern was already here, and she was the only one who couldn't see it. Her jaw locked. If she couldn't see it, she couldn't stop it. And if she couldn't stop it...

A voice cut through the mist. "I told you... I felt it coming."

Claire jerked upright, spinning toward the sound.

Nessa stood just beyond the tape, half-silhouetted in the glare. Her auburn hair clung in damp strands, plastered to her cheek. She wasn't wearing a hood. The rain slicked across her as if she hadn't noticed or didn't care.

Claire's pulse kicked hard, though her voice came out steady.

"Nessa."

Nessa tilted her head; eyes fixed on the slick patch of road where Jacob had lain. "The air's still heavy with it," she murmured.

"This is a crime scene," Claire said, irritation rising fast to mask the chill under her skin. "What are you doing here?"

"I had to come." Nessa's gaze drifted over the cracked pavement and fading skid marks. "The darkness was here. I could feel it."

Her voice was soft, but it cut through the mist.

Claire's grip tightened on her flashlight. "Feel it," she echoed, sharper than she intended.

Nessa's eyes finally lifted to hers, gleaming faintly. "The roads remember. They always remember who they crown... and who they take back.”

Something cold slipped down Claire’s spine.

She opened her mouth, but no words came. A part of her wanted to dismiss it as theatrics. Another part, the part she hated, wondered if Nessa was seeing something she couldn’t.

Before she could speak, footsteps sounded behind her.

“Detective Sandoval,” Liam said, brisk but worn. “It’s the same, isn’t it?”

“This is a restricted area,” Claire warned.

He crouched near the spoke. “That’s the fifth one. Same message.”

Nessa tilted her head toward him. “You want to know what it wants.”

Liam frowned. “What does it want?”

“It’s not about killing,” she said. “It’s about breaking something. Leaving a mark that doesn’t fade.”

Claire stepped closer. “If you know something, Nessa, speak plainly.”

“It repeats. The road remembers. It finds cracks in people and widens them.”

Liam's tone hardened. "You talk like the road is alive."

"It's not the road," she declared. "It's people. That's what makes it worse."

"Why do you know so much about this?" Claire asked.

"Because I've seen it," Nessa replied, her voice barely above a whisper.

Liam stepped forward. "Why are you here?"

Her gaze moved to the spoke. "Because someone has to see the truth."

Claire folded her arms. "Then give me something useful."

"You see a crime scene," Nessa murmured. "I see what is left behind."

She turned and walked into the mist, her voice floating back. "Be careful, Detective. And you, Mr. Harper. The darkness isn't just after them. It's after anyone who dares to chase it."

Liam watched her vanish between the trees.

"She's either the most insightful person in this town or completely gone."

"Maybe both," Claire said. "But we can't ignore her."

Liam crouched again, studying the spoke. "This wasn't rushed. Whoever's doing this takes their time."

Claire's attention returned to the road. "This isn't just murder. It's a fracture. And Havenport's starting to break."

The words clung to him.

He stepped back from the tape as the floodlights hissed and hummed, halos of pale light dissolving into the mist. The ground smelled of oil, rain, and something sour beneath. The breeze shifted, and the distant crash of waves bled faintly through the trees, a rhythm out of sync with everything around him.

He shoved his notebook into his jacket and walked to his car, boots crunching softly over the damp gravel.

By the time Millie's neon sign came into view down the empty stretch of road, he knew he wouldn't go inside yet.

Instead, he sat in the driver's seat under the glow of the sign, engine ticking as it cooled. The chatter from inside was barely audible through the glass, a distant, hollow murmur. The kind of sound people made when they were pretending everything was fine.

He opened his notebook across his knee. The pages were warped from humidity; the edges curled and softened. Names stared back at him from older notes: Victor, Elliot, Megan, Derek, Jacob; inked in his quick, jagged scrawl.

He wrote them again in a clean column, slower this time, his pen dragging a little from the damp air.

Victor - Control. He could still picture the crispness of his posture, his voice clipped even mid-ride, the way others deferred to him without question.

Elliot - Arrogance. Always attacking from the start line, grinning like rules were suggestions.

Megan - Light. She had been the warmth that made the group work, her laughter filling the dead air after long climbs.

Derek - Rhythm. Steady and methodical, the metronome was unnoticed until it stopped.

His pen hovered over Jacob's name.

What had Jacob been to them?

Not the strongest. Not the loudest. Just... constant. The one who stayed when everyone else slipped away. The one who made them believe staying was possible.

Comfort, he wrote at last.

The word looked wrong on the page. Too soft. Too human.

A faint pressure settled behind his sternum, something like dread curling inward. If someone was choosing them for what they represented, this wasn't random.

He set the pen down carefully, as if the thought might splinter if he moved too fast.

Through the diner window, he could see Millie pouring coffee, her motions sharp and mechanical. A group of regulars sat huddled at the counter, talking too quietly, their eyes darting toward the door like they half-expected Jacob to walk in.

Liam closed the notebook. His fingers lingered on the cover.

For weeks, he had told himself he was just chronicling this. Recording facts, collecting quotes, and staying objective. But tonight, staring at that column of names, he felt the shape of something closing around him.

He slid the notebook back into his jacket and opened the door. The air hit cold and damp as he stepped out, boots crunching on the wet pavement.

The neon hum grew louder as he walked toward the diner's glow. Millie's counter was where whispers turned into truth. And he needed the truth.

The bell above the diner door jingled, a cheerful sound that didn't fit the mood. Inside, conversation dulled. Morning chatter had been replaced by muted voices and cautious glances.

Millie stood behind the counter, pouring coffee with practiced hands. Her face stayed calm, but her expression gave her worry away.

"Millie," Liam said, sliding onto a stool and nodding toward the pot.

She filled a cup and set it down. "Heard you were out by Route 7," she said. "Jacob was a good man."

Liam nodded and took a sip. "Doesn't get easier."

He flipped open his notebook. "What have you heard?"

Millie leaned in slightly. "He was at Haven Café yesterday. Sat with a couple of the riders. Pete saw him. Said Jacob kept glancing over his shoulder, like someone was following him."

She paused. "Didn't think much of it then. But now?"

Liam jotted notes. "Anything about what they talked about?"

"The race. They're trying to act normal, but you can feel it; they're rattled," Millie said. "Some folks think it's a curse. An old one."

Liam underlined the word curse.

"Anyone strange hanging around?"

Millie shook her head. "Just locals. But fear makes even the familiar look strange."

Erin, a young cyclist, slid into the seat beside him. Her voice was low. "You're covering this for the paper, right?"

Liam nodded. "I am. Did Jacob tell you anything?"

She hesitated. "He said he was seeing things. He mentioned something out near the quarry." Her voice dropped even lower. "He thought he saw the Ghost Rider."

Millie stilled, the coffee pot frozen midair. "The quarry," she murmured. "That place breeds stories. Maybe too many."

Frank approached and rested a hand on Liam's shoulder. "If you think Jacob's death was an accident, you're wrong. Someone's picking us off. Starting with the pros, then the ones who know the roads best."

"You think it's intentional?" Liam asked.

Frank's jaw tightened. "It's a twisted routine. And until we figure it out, no one's safe."

Liam scribbled: *ritual, specific riders, order unknown.*

Millie spoke again, her voice barely above a whisper. "You think this ties to the old stories? About the lighthouse, or the quarry?"

Liam hesitated. "Maybe. Jacob believed something was out there. Whether it's a person or fear itself, someone's using those stories."

The diner went still. Even the clink of cups sounded distant.

Liam drained his coffee and closed his notebook. "Thanks, Millie. Erin, Frank," he nodded. "I'll keep digging."

As he stepped into the cold, he glanced back through the window. The quiet inside clung to him as he drove toward the community center, replaying the words in his head: curse, ritual, Ghost Rider. Each clue felt close, almost within reach, but too slippery to hold.

He parked beside the low brick building off Main Street. The air outside was dense, the light barely rising. Mist curled around the tires as he stepped out.

Inside, the center was hushed; faint voices carried from down the hallway, blending with the squeak of chairs on tile. A bulletin board near the entrance displayed flyers for local races and fundraisers. The normalcy of it all felt off, like a backdrop that no longer matched the reality of Havenport.

In the main room, Liam spotted Sam and Jen leaning over a table littered with maps, route plans, and training schedules. Sam looked up, managing a tired smile.

"Liam," Sam said. "Figured you'd show up. This one's hitting everyone hard."

Liam joined them, setting his notebook on the table. "People can't stop talking about Jacob. It feels like something's closing in on the cycling community."

Jen's arms crossed tightly. "It's not just talk. There's something wrong. Last night I went for a ride and could've sworn someone was watching from the trees."

Sam glanced at her with mild irritation. "Or maybe we're all on edge because the town's spinning rumors faster than facts."

Jen shot him a look. "You think Jacob just fell? You know better. He didn't scare easily."

Sam let out a slow breath, rubbing his jaw. "I'm not saying it wasn't deliberate. But this feels like more than ghost stories or whatever nonsense people are whispering."

Liam's pen hovered over the page. "What do you think it is, then?"

"Politics," Sam said. "Jacob's been caught in the middle of the old racers and the new riders. The race schedule has been a mess this season. Permits, route disputes, and sponsorship fights, he stepped on toes."

Jen shook her head, her voice sharp. "That's not it, Sam. Jacob wasn't the type to make enemies over something like that."

Sam's tone hardened. "You don't know everyone's grudges. You think people don't carry resentment? Victor, Elliot, Megan, Derek, and Jacob... they were all names that meant something. That kind of spotlight draws jealousy."

Liam glanced between them, sensing the history in the way they argued. "Did Jacob mention anyone specific? Any disputes?"

Jen's mouth tightened. "He was more worried about the mood around town. Said it felt like everyone was riding with a chip on their shoulder. But he never named names."

Sam tapped the map with two fingers, tracing a route near the quarry. "He mentioned someone following him out there last week. Said they were close enough to hear his gears shift. But I think it was just another rider who didn't want to be seen."

"That's a big assumption," Jen snapped.

Sam looked straight at her. "I'm trying to keep this grounded. If we go chasing ghost riders and curses, we'll miss what's right in front of us."

Jen looked away, her jaw tight. "Sometimes what's right in front of us is worse than a curse."

Liam jotted down quarry, lighthouse, and grudges. "Did he feel threatened?"

Jen hesitated. "He didn't say it out loud. But he changed. Stuck more to the main roads. That wasn't Jacob."

Sam leaned back, frustration etched into his face.

"These aren't random accidents. But I'm not convinced this is about legends. It's personal. Someone knows this community inside and out."

Liam closed his notebook. The soft snap of it shutting seemed to pull the air from the room. No one spoke.

Sam's words hung there, dense and heavy, like a storm cloud sagging under its own rain.

Liam rose quietly, chair legs scraping faintly on the worn tile. He nodded a vague goodbye, though no one really looked up.

Once outside, the door closed behind him with a hollow thud. A gust of wind cut through his coat, sharp with the bite of salt air. The night was still, the streets washed in dull pools of neon and rainlight, but something in the town's shape felt... different. Off-kilter.

The buildings were the same. The roads stretched exactly where they always had. But standing there in the damp silence, Liam realized they no longer looked like routes. They looked like scars.

7

The Tangled Veil

The light slipped away, thin across the streets. Old Victorian houses stood tall, their chipped shutters and weathered bricks whispering of lives long past. It felt as if the street itself was keeping watch.

Beyond them, the cliffs fell into the Atlantic. The ocean, usually restless, was muted by the heavy mist that clung to the shore, moving as though it knew to tread carefully.

Detective Sandoval stood alone in the main square. She looked down the narrow streets where cycling trails wound through the pines. The burden of the murders, her mind churning through the puzzle: the victims, the broken spokes, Nessa's cryptic warnings. Too many pieces refused to fit.

A sudden sound broke through. Footsteps. Claire turned to see Ryan Moore.

His tall, athletic frame was immediately recognizable, lit in slivers by the fractured glow of a nearby streetlamp. A half-zipped cycling jacket clung to his shoulders, a faint neon stripe glowing like a pulse. His hair, damp with sweat, curled slightly at the edges.

"Claire," he said cautiously. "Didn't expect to see you here."

A flicker of irritation crossed her mind, but it didn't land. It was chased too quickly by a strange warmth that caught her off guard.

"Same goes for you," she replied, her voice edged but not cold. "What brings you out here?"

He stepped closer. "Needed to clear my head," he said. "Riding in weather like this... It's like slipping into another world."

"Or hiding from the real one," she said. "What are you running from, Ryan?"

He didn't smile this time. "You, of all people, should under-stand why someone might need to escape." His voice had dropped. "I'm not running. I'm trying to understand what's happening here."

Claire shifted her weight but didn't step back.

"Then help me understand," she said. "You've been tangled in this from the start. First with Marissa, now with the victims. I need to know how deep this goes."

Ryan's jaw tightened. "Marissa and I... that's over," he said. "You're right, though. I knew the victims. I was part of their world. Still am, I guess."

Claire felt her pulse pick up, just slightly. "What aren't you telling me? Is there more to Marissa than you've said?"

Frustration passed over his face, but beneath it was something else. Regret.

"I'm not protecting Marissa," he said. "Not anymore. We haven't talked since the accident. She pushed everyone away. Including me."

"Then why keep it to yourself?" Claire asked. "Your past with her. How close you were to all of them."

He exhaled slowly. "Because I was ashamed. Not of her, of me. Of how long I stayed silent."

She didn't respond.

"Back then," he went on, "we were just misfits on bikes. No structure. No ego. Just... freedom."

His voice turned softer. "Then things changed. Got serious. Competitive. Marissa wanted out, said it was turning ugly. She was right."

"What happened?" Claire asked.

"She walked out. On all of us, on me. And I let her."

He looked at her, dark with memory. "I didn't fight for her. I didn't say what I should have. I kept the peace instead of standing up. And it broke something between us. Between all of us."

Claire tilted her head, studying him. She was beginning to see the cracks he rarely let show.

Ryan's voice thickened. "That night never stopped following me. And it's not just about Marissa. It's who I became after. Always watching, always reporting; but never standing in the line of fire."

He looked at her then, really looked at her. "You do. You take the hits. I admire that about you."

Claire's voice dropped. "So why now? Why tell me this tonight?"

"Because I trust you," he said. "And because I'm tired of being the guy who holds the truth and does nothing with it."

The streetlight above them flickered. He drew in a slow breath, like he was about to say something heavier, something personal.

"There was a time I thought I'd be next," he said quietly. "It passed... or maybe it just moved on. Sometimes I still wonder why."

His gaze drifted past her, unfocused, then sharpened again.

"Doesn't matter," he said, too quickly.

"You say you care," Claire said softly. "But caring and telling the truth aren't always the same thing."

"I know." He stepped closer, just enough that she had to tilt her chin to look at his face. "I'm trying to be both. But I'm starting to realize... I might not get to keep both."

A long pause passed between them. Claire could feel something unspoken but alive between them.

"If you want to help," she said, her voice barely above a whisper, "you know where to start."

Ryan nodded, then hesitated. "I'll go back to the group. Ask the questions no one wants to ask."

He looked down at her hand, then into her eyes. "But Claire... if this leads where I think it might, the truth won't bring peace. It's going to wreck people."

Her breath slowed, but she didn't look away. "Wreck it anyway."

For a moment, neither of them moved. Ryan's fingers lightly touched her wrist, a fleeting pause that spoke more than words. Claire didn't pull back.

"I don't know where this ends," he said, "but I'm not staying silent anymore."

She watched him go, not as someone retreating, but as someone choosing to step into the light. The warmth of his touch stayed with her. Claire remained, watching the fog fold around Ryan. Even the mist seemed to hesitate around him, as if it understood the cost of truth.

Ryan stood where all the broken pieces seemed to meet. Where grief, suspicion, and hope collided and refused to separate.

Was he truly an ally, or just another story wrapped in half-truths?

The thought slipped through her chest, and with it came the familiar shadow of the overdose case. Not the reports or the press briefings, the silence. The hollow space where a girl had been, and Claire's certainty had failed her.

She had waited for a pattern then, too. Waiting for the chaos to change itself into something she could understand. It never did.

The fear slid cold through her now: what if this was the same? What if the pattern existed, and she was blind to it again?

The case wasn't loosening. It was digging in, burrowing deeper into her with every loss.

She turned from the path and scanned the cliffs, then the empty streets. She was searching, not just for a suspect, but for the shape of something hiding beneath fear; before it slipped through her fingers again.

Behind her, she heard footsteps. Claire turned to see Liam Harper approaching, his notebook tucked under his arm, shoulders squared.

"Didn't think anyone else would be out here," he said as he joined her.

Claire gave a small nod. "You've got a way of finding the tension."

A faint smile flickered. "Bad habit. Comes with the job."

She looked at his notebook. "What have you got?"

"Stopped by Millie's," Liam said, flipping it open. The pages were rippled from the mist, corners softened by the damp. "Jacob's name is everywhere. Millie said he was at Haven Café yesterday, sitting alone. Erin saw him too. Said he looked... off. Like he was somewhere else entirely."

Claire's brow furrowed. "He didn't usually ride solo."

"Exactly." Liam tapped his notes, the click of his pen sharp in the fog. "And Erin said the Ghost Rider talk is hotter than ever. Riders are whispering that it's not just a story anymore. Some think it's personal, revenge, maybe."

Claire looked past him, drawn to the dark line of trees where the lights faded into shadow. "It was just folklore. Until now."

"There's more," Liam said. "I hit the community center after. Sam and Jen were there with the race maps. Both said Jacob seemed on edge. Jen swears he thought someone was watching him. Frank's been saying the same; he thinks old grudges are surfacing again, stuff that goes way back."

Claire's expression tightened. "Grudges don't die easily, especially around here."

"People are changing their routines," Liam added. "Riding in pairs, sticking to daylight. Like they know something but can't put words to it."

Claire exhaled slowly, watching her breath vanish. "A group like that doesn't spook over rumors. If Jacob was nervous, he felt something real. Maybe more than he said out loud."

Liam's pen hovered over the page. "You think he knew he was a target?"

"I think he knew someone was," she said. "And he went out alone anyway."

Liam hesitated, thumb tracing the edge of the page. His voice softened. "Can I ask something off the record?"

Claire turned to him. "You can ask. Doesn't mean I'll answer."

He offered a faint smile. "Fair."

His tone shifted. "Do you think the Ghost Rider, whoever it is, is real? Not just a name for fear?"

Claire didn't answer right away. The night around them seemed to pause.

"If it's real," she said at last, "it's not a ghost. It's someone who knows these roads, the habits, the people. It's personal. Precise."

"And fear does the rest."

"Exactly. Fear works faster than facts."

Liam glanced down at his notes, thumb brushing the edge of a page covered in scattered names. His voice lowered, more to himself than to her.

"I've been trying to find the thread. Victor, Elliot, Megan, Derek, now Jacob... they weren't random. Each one held something the others leaned on. Control. Bravado. Light. Rhythm. And Jacob... he was comfort. The kind that makes people think the world can't crack."

Claire's eyes glanced at him. There was something in his tone now, less like reporting, more like warning. "You think someone's dismantling them."

"I think someone's proving they can," he said, the words steady.

"So, what now?" he asked after a moment.

"We push harder," Claire said. "Friends, rivals, teammates. We ask what no one wants to answer. Even if it costs us goodwill."

"You think we're close?"

"Close enough to scare someone," she said.

They stood there for a long moment, the mist curling around their feet, the road stretching silent and dark in both directions.

"You're not just chasing quotes anymore, are you?" she asked.

"Not when it's this close to home."

Claire gave a brief nod, and Liam closed the notebook. Whatever was circling this town, it had just drawn them deeper.

Liam glanced once more at the empty road. Under his breath, he mouthed their names again. Then he turned and walked back toward the lights.

Night fell over Havenport, cloaking the town in darkness that softened edges but sharpened awareness. Beneath the calm, something older stirred, not with urgency, but with purpose.

The town believed the story was the beginning. The truth was harder to face. This wasn't the start. It was only the moment people began to notice. The pieces had been falling for much longer.

Victor's fall drew attention, but it was only part of the design. He carried authority without questioning it. People trusted him, and he liked that. He built a life on control. But control, left unchecked, can make you blind.

Victor once said, "Without structure, a rider is just spinning wheels."

He never asked who built the road beneath him. He believed he was creating something noble. He wasn't. His influence boxed people in, drew lines, and he expected them to color inside them.

Taking him down wasn't revenge. It was clean, calm, and precise. Remove the frame, and the rest collapses.

Elliot's danger lived close to the surface. He moved like someone who was always being chased. People admired his speed, mistaking it for fearlessness. But speed blurs the truth. He wasn't running from danger; he was running from himself.

He flew down hills like fear was behind him, but it was always inside. His crash wasn't shocking; the calm after was. Everyone saw it coming, but they looked away.

Megan was harder; her kindness was real. She calmed rooms. But peace can be dangerous. She didn't lie; she helped people avoid the truth. That was her gift and her flaw. She believed keeping the peace was enough. But peace without truth is numbness.

Her absence left people adrift. Not because she commanded them, but because she anchored them. Without her, the illusion unraveled.

Derek was the calm center, carrying the truth no one wanted to face. He fixed things and kept the surface smooth. But steadiness built on silence cracks. It looks fine until the foundation fails. His death didn't just hurt. It shook the structure.

Jacob was different. He didn't lead, and he didn't follow. He watched. He was starting to see the pattern. He understood more than he said. Maybe too much. He believed silence would protect him. It didn't. Clarity without action isolates you. It makes you stand out. He was getting close, too close. So, he was removed before he could speak.

None of these losses stands alone. Each one tilts the balance, loosens another thread. The roles that once held this place together are fraying; not from outside, but from within.

Now the fear isn't just about who's next. It's about what's already gone, and what the unraveling is exposing.

They call it the Ghost Rider. A legend. A story. But legends don't move with precision. Stories don't know the bends in the road, the places the wind cuts hardest.

This isn't a ghost, it's intention. Someone who sees what lies beneath the surface. Someone who remembers what this town chooses to forget.

Ryan was supposed to be next. He fit the shape of it; steady, visible, the one they circle as if his balance might keep theirs from breaking. And for a moment, he almost was. He felt the shadow pass over him. Knew it, even if he never named it.

But Ryan didn't crack. He bent. He held fast to the edges and refused to fall.

There's no use in breaking what won't shatter cleanly. The wheel kept turning. And now, it points to someone else.

8

The Unraveling Path

The bell above the door rang out, crisp and jarring in the stillness. Marissa looked up from her work, not startled, but watchful. Her expression was composed, unreadable. Behind her calm, something braced itself.

Liam stepped into the shop, moving with the self-assurance of someone who liked walking close to the edge.

"Back so soon?" Marissa asked, not looking up from the brake assembly she was adjusting.

"You know me," Liam said with a smile. "Always chasing a better version of the truth."

"I thought you already got what you came for."

"Not even close," he said. "Last time, we skimmed the surface. This time I want the current."

Marissa set the wrench down and turned slightly toward him. "And you think you'll find that here? In a broken-down bike shop with a woman, you've already written off as bitter and irrelevant?"

"Not irrelevant," Liam replied. "Deeply connected. The people who died were all part of your world once."

Marissa's jaw clenched. "A world I left behind a long time ago."

"Did you? You're still here."

"That doesn't mean I'm part of it."

"But it means you see it," Liam said, stepping closer. "You see what's been changing. You know who held the power, who cracked under it, who was left behind."

"Careful, Liam. You're starting to sound like a conspiracy theorist."

He tilted his head. "Or maybe just a journalist paying atten-tion."

She stared at him for a long moment. "You want a quote for your story? Here it is. People crash. People burn out. And eventually, people forget."

"But you haven't," Liam responded.

"No," Marissa admitted. "I haven't. But that doesn't mean I'm involved."

"You were a top contender once. Before the crash."

She flinched. Just slightly. "Don't pretend you understand what that meant."

"I'm not pretending. I'm asking what it cost you."

Marissa didn't answer. Instead, she wiped her hands clean and stared down at the gears in front of her. "You think I'm hiding something."

"I think you're guarding it. There's a difference."

She exhaled through her nose. "And what exactly is it you think I'm guarding?"

"The past. Someone else. Maybe even yourself."

"You think this is about me?"

"I think you're tired. And you don't like being seen."

Marissa turned to face him fully now. "You think you can stand in here and read me like a page from one of your columns?"

"No," he said. "But I know the look of someone carrying something they never put down."

There was a long pause.

"You want to know why I stay?" she asked. "Why I'm still here, fixing bikes in a town that chewed me up and spit me out?"

"Yes," Liam said.

"Because maybe," she said, "I'm trying to repair something I couldn't hold together back then."

Liam studied her, the hardness in his features giving way to something more careful.

"Or maybe," he said, "you're waiting for someone else to do what you couldn't."

Marissa's hands stopped.

"Don't psychoanalyze me, Liam," she said. "You don't know what you're digging into."

"I don't," he agreed. "But I think you do. And you're terrified of what might happen if someone else sees it too."

Marissa stared at him, something unreadable on her face.

"And what about you?" she asked. "Why chase ghosts, Liam? What's this really about?"

"Closure," he said. "Same as you."

The silence between them was strong.

Marissa turned back to the bike, her voice low. "You should go."

Liam didn't argue. He walked to the door, his voice muted as he pushed it open. "I'll be back. You already know that."

She didn't respond.

As the door shut behind him, the sound echoed through the small shop. Marissa didn't look up. Her fingers tightened on the handlebars in front of her.

She closed the shop earlier than usual. A restlessness pushed her toward the street, where the cold air bit through her jacket. The usual chatter of cyclists had faded, leaving behind a silence the town no longer recognized.

She glanced toward the woods, her gaze holding on to the dark trails she once rode. They weren't just memories. They stayed with her, like chapters in a story she hadn't finished but somehow understood all too well.

The smell of wet pine brought it back: the blur of the descent, the shriek of twisting metal, and the air tearing from her lungs as the world flipped. She remembered the taste of dirt and blood, the sound of voices shouting her name as if from underwater, and the hollow certainty that her body had become wreckage.

Everyone else had called it an accident. She had called it the end. But it never really ended. It only lingered, waiting.

Across town, Liam walked alone beneath the dim glow of the streetlamps, his notebook tucked under his arm. He remembered her words, her guarded eyes, and the way her hands had tightened when he pressed too close. He had wanted to believe he was collecting truths; documenting, not disturbing. But that line felt thinner.

Marissa had once been part of the same machine he was now trying to map. It had broken her. And he couldn't shake the thought that by digging deep enough, by pulling at the same threads, he might be feeding the gears instead of exposing them.

A faint wind shifted through the trees, carrying the smell of salt and cold metal. He kept walking.

Not far beyond those trees, hidden in the dense undergrowth, something waited. It wasn't a clue in the traditional sense, no fingerprints or trail of evidence, just a soft shift in the air. A silent presence woven into the landscape. Not loud, undeniable. Not a message, exactly, more like a decision already made. The path ahead curved into the gloom, and at the end of it stood Lena Crawford.

Lena, with her open smile and perfect posture, would never see it coming. There was a cadence to her routine. Her rides carved the same path each day, tracing familiar routes with muscle memory. Even her joy felt rehearsed.

She pedaled along cliffside roads with unshakable optimism, completely unaware of how dangerous her predictability had become. Her confidence wasn't naïve. It was infuriating.

The night moved with purpose. Silent and precise, like the blade of a scalpel. The air carried a charge that didn't belong. No wind, no storm. Something more primal. It shimmered beneath the surface of things. Lena's days were numbered.

Every detail had been studied. What time she brewed her coffee, who she waved to on morning rides, and how long she paused before descending the hill behind her building. She hummed when she thought no one was listening. These things mattered; they were pieces of the script.

Down the narrow alley beside Lena's apartment, a silhouette paused beneath her kitchen window. Inside, the light glowed soft and golden. She moved through her evening as always. Tea poured into her favorite mug, helmet by the door, keys on the hook. All of it still. All of it known.

The ritual was nearly complete. Each of them followed one. That was the key. They moved through life on repeat. And that was what made it so easy, their habits and comfort. Their blind spots. Lena's final ride had already been written. It would unfold without her even realizing.

The figure slipped away from the window, disappearing back into the night. Morning came like any other.

Lena moved through her kitchen, the gentle hum of the

coffeemaker filling the silence. She poured herself a mug, inhaled the familiar warmth, and looked out the window with contentment.

At the edge of her yard, just beyond the reach of the morning light, a shadow lingered. Motionless and watching. It had been there for almost an hour, waiting, learning. Every movement Lena made was predictable. Every choice was expected. She was a pattern playing out in real time.

She placed the mug in the sink, pulled on her jacket, and clipped her helmet. Then she stepped out into the cold, unaware she was no longer alone. Her neon windbreaker caught the pale dawn light as she mounted her bike and began to pedal down the street.

The wheels turned effortlessly. Her body moved by instinct, gliding over the pavement. She didn't rush or hesitate. It was a ride she had done a hundred times.

The roads opened up, empty and still. As she passed into the wooded section near Snake Hollow, her speed increased. The descent began, smooth and familiar. Her hands hovered lightly on the brakes. She smiled at herself.

Down the winding trail, her bright jacket flickered through the trees. She coasted through the bends, oblivious to how far she'd come from safety. The landscape wrapped around her, indifferent to what was coming. She had no idea she was riding straight into it.

Lately, the whole town had begun to move at a different pace. Slower, more hesitant. People shared looks in the grocery store and paused longer on porches. The cyclists, especially. They scanned their surroundings at every turn, as if danger had taken on a new shape.

It had.

And Lena entered. Her figure cut bright against the dim woods, a flash of color against the dimness. She rode hard, unguarded, the way they all once did. Her silhouette thinned and vanished around the final bend.

Soon, the silence returned. Leaves stirred overhead as the figure stepped from the trees, moving back onto the path, each footfall soft and deliberate.

They had been close; close enough to see the rhythm of her breath, the looseness in her shoulders, and the trust she still carried in her speed.

But this was not the moment. Not yet.

A branch snapped in the distance, but no one looked. The roads were waking up with cautious motion, but most still rode with blind confidence, clinging to the illusion that if they kept moving fast enough, fear couldn't catch them.

By midmorning, sunlight broke through the clouds, revealing the edges of Havenport's center. Cyclists looped past the square; their movements were stiffer than normal. Jittery.

Near the fountain, Nessa stood alone, a cigarette between her fingers, the smoke curling around her. She tracked every flash of reflective gear that cut through the mist. There was no hiding her contempt.

Ryan slowed as he passed the old hardware store, catching the tail end of a conversation between two men hunched on a bench. Their voices were low, meant for each other.

"Once they crowned a king of the roads," one of them muttered. "And the roads took him back."

The other just nodded, staring at the wet cobblestones like they might crack.

Ryan kept walking, their words sliding under his skin. He spotted Nessa from down the block and hesitated before crossing. He noticed the tense set of her shoulders and the way her eyes followed the passing cyclists, as if she were deciphering something invisible to everyone else.

The smoke from her cigarette curled up and shredded in the breeze, vanishing before it reached the sunlight.

"Nessa," he called gently, stepping up beside her. "You've been out here a while."

She didn't answer right away. The tip of her cigarette burned a little brighter before she finally flicked the ash and exhaled. Her gaze stayed fixed on the road, following the spinning wheels until they disappeared.

"Town feels different, doesn't it?" she murmured.

Ryan studied her profile, the sharpness of her cheekbones against the gray light. "Yeah. Feels like everyone's holding their breath."

Nessa's mouth twitched, almost a smile, though nothing warm lived in it. "They used to ride like they owned the roads. Like the roads owed them something."

Ryan frowned. "And now?"

"Now they ride like the roads are keeping score."

She turned her head then, just enough that her eyes met his. There was a strange clarity in them, something bright and wise.

"Things break when they forget what carries them," she said softly. "And the roads... they never forget."

Ryan shifted his weight, uneasy. "You make it sound like they deserve what's happening."

"Deserves got nothing to do with it." Her voice sharpened, sudden and cold. "Balance does."

"Balance?"

She dropped the cigarette and crushed it under her boot. "Maybe it's about time they remembered they're not untouchable."

Then she turned sharply and walked off, coat flaring with the motion.

Ryan watched her go, the sharp scent of her cigarette still hanging in the air. Her words clung to him; blunt, unapologetic, and far too specific to ignore.

He stood there for a moment longer, struck by the certainty in her tone. She wasn't just spouting opinions. She sounded like someone who knew what was coming.

He turned and made his way to Haven Café, their conversation replaying in his mind. As he stepped into the warmth of the Café, the smell of fresh coffee and pastries greeted him like a memory. It should have brought comfort, but even here, the usual buzz had thinned.

Conversations were hushed, and laughter was gone. Fear had made itself a regular. People looked up as he entered, staring a little too long. Not in recognition, but suspicion. As if he might be closer to the truth than he let on.

He slid into a booth by the window, scanning the street outside. Steam spread across the glass in slow circles, mirroring the uncertainty creeping through his mind. Nessa's words kept circling back, louder than he wanted. Her pleasure in the town's fear. Her talk of reckoning and cycles snapping back into place. She wasn't just indulging in a morbid fascination. She believed in what was happening.

A mug of coffee appeared in front of him. Erin dropped into the seat across from him without asking.

"Saw you with Nessa in the square," she said, her voice low. "She's been... different."

Ryan raised a brow. "How so?"

"She's everywhere lately. Watching people. Talking about punishment like it's personal." Erin glanced around the room, then leaned closer. "I heard her yesterday telling someone the Ghost Rider isn't a myth. That it's real and here."

Ryan frowned. "And what? That he's cleaning up the town?"

Erin nodded slowly. "She said he's restoring balance, like this is all some kind of correction. It gave me chills."

Ryan stared down into his coffee, the steam curling between them. Nessa's words at the fountain kept circling back; about riders who once thought the roads owed them something, and how they were keeping score now. About things breaking when people forget what carries them. *Balance*, she'd said, sharp and certain. Not anger. Not vengeance. Balance.

"She's got her reasons," he murmured. "I don't think she's behind it, but she's wicked close to the truth. Too close."

"You think she's connected?" Erin asked, a tremor in her voice.

"Not directly," he said slowly. "But maybe she knows who is, or she's part of the story and doesn't even realize it."

They sat in silence; the sounds of the café were dull around them.

Ryan's hand tightened around the mug. "Whatever this is," he said, "it's not random. And Nessa's not just talking for the thrill of it. She knows something. She's always watching. And I think she's waiting for us to figure it out."

Erin looked out the window. "Or for someone to stop asking questions."

Ryan didn't respond.

III

Web of Deceit

9

The Line Between Trust and Fear

Detective Sandoval pulled up outside the Haven Café. Inside, the regulars sat with lowered voices and wary faces. Conversations paused when someone new walked in. What used to be a place of routine now felt like a room full of questions she didn't yet have answers to. She stepped out of the car and headed for the door.

Claire spotted him immediately. Ryan was seated at his usual booth by the window, the light catching the side of his face. He looked up as she entered, his expression unreadable at first; then warm, but cautious. That mix again. Curious, connected. Dangerous.

"Morning," she said, sliding into the seat across from him.

Ryan studied her. "Back for more questions?"

"You know me," she replied, managing a faint smile. "Unanswered questions are a bad habit."

He leaned back slightly. "Let me guess... this is about Marissa?"

"It does keep circling back to her. She's at the center, whether she wants to be or not."

Ryan's smile faded. "You're chasing ghosts, Claire. She's not the villain in this story."

"She's not just a bystander either," Claire said. "You've seen it. The way she's changed. That bitterness; it's not harmless."

"She lost everything," Ryan said. "She was betrayed by her own body. That kind of loss breaks people."

"Or remakes them," Claire replied. "Sometimes into something darker."

His fingers traced the edge of his coffee mug. "You don't know her like I do."

"I'm starting to wonder if you do," Claire said. "You've been careful, Ryan. Careful with what you say. With what you don't say."

He didn't flinch. "Because I know how this works. One wrong word and suddenly you're the next person in the crosshairs."

Claire leaned forward, voice low. "Then tell me the right words. Help me understand what you're not saying."

He didn't look away. Then, slowly, he reached forward, not in some grand gesture, but with a sweet tenderness. A single strand of her hair had fallen loose, and he brushed it back behind her ear. His touch rested for just a second too long, his fingertips warm against her temple.

"You're always chasing the truth," he said, almost a whisper. "But sometimes it's closer than you think."

Claire didn't move. The contact had been fleeting. Her body stiffened, not in resistance, but in confusion; she wasn't sure whether she wanted to lean in or pull away.

"Ryan..." she began.

He cut her off gently. "You're trying to do your job and trying to keep your heart out of it. That's not going to work. Not with me."

The words struck deep. Claire's walls were built for protection, but Ryan's presence always found cracks. She was silent for a moment.

"Be honest with me, Ryan," she said finally. "I can handle the truth. Whatever it is."

He nodded, slowly. "I will, Claire. Just remember, sometimes the truth doesn't set you free. Sometimes, it binds you tighter."

She rose from the booth without a word; her coat draped over one arm. The café door creaked open as she stepped into the cold.

Ryan stayed seated, staring into the swirl of his coffee. Her reflection had slipped out of the glass, leaving only his own, faint and doubled. The café hummed softly around him, the clink of cups and the low murmur of voices folding back into place, but it all sounded distant, as though it belonged to another world.

Victor. Elliot. Megan. Derek. Jacob. Their names drifted through his mind like shadows on the tide.

He had been at the center of them all, orbiting the same races, the same roads, the same sharp edges of ambition. And somehow, he was still here. Sometimes he wondered if that made him lucky or just marked, like the current had swept everyone else away and left him stranded.

He turned the mug in his hands. Steam curled and vanished before it touched his face. He tried to remember what it felt like to ride without looking over his shoulder, to breathe without feeling names press against his lungs. There had been a time when riding meant freedom, when the world narrowed to wind and wheels and nothing else. Now every mile carries ghosts.

He could not shake the sense that something had been following him. It came in flashes: the prickle between his shoulder blades, the shape that never formed when he glanced back, the soft shift of air when the road should have been still.

It was as though the killer had marked him once and then changed their mind, slipping away before the strike. That thought clung to him more tightly than the near-misses he had survived on the bike. There were moments on the quiet roads at dawn, when the mist sank low and the world had not yet woken, when he could hear another pair of tires behind him. Not loud. Steady and waiting.

And then there was Marissa. She had once been the person who rode just ahead of him, pulling him forward with a glance over her shoulder and a crooked grin that dared him to keep up. He had been young enough to believe that would never change, that her fire would carry her forever.

When she fell, it rewrote everything. He told himself he had kept his distance out of respect, but part of him knew it had been fear. If someone like her could be broken, anyone could. Even him. Especially him.

Claire unsettled him differently. She carried the storm inside her, yet she moved through it like someone who expected to reach the other side. There were moments she looked at him like he was part of the chaos she was trying to solve, and other moments she looked at him like he was the only quiet place left. He could not decide which unnerved him more. She made him want to be honest, but honesty always came with a cost.

Survivor's guilt was supposed to fade. It had not. If anything, it had settled deeper, in the hollow spaces the silence had left behind. It shaped how people flinched when he walked into a room. It shaped how he caught himself wondering, more often than he wanted to admit, why he was still here when the others were not.

Outside, Claire paused on the sidewalk, the chill crawling across her skin. She glanced back through the window. Ryan hadn't moved. She didn't know what scared her more, that he might be lying, or that he might finally be telling the truth.

Her mind was a tangle of emotion and instinct, frayed edges catching on each other until nothing felt certain. That one brief gesture from him had slipped past her guard, leaving a dull ache she didn't want to name. It wasn't just about Ryan anymore. It was about the storm gathering inside her, the sense that every choice she made from here could tip something she could never reset.

She stopped by her car and let her hands rest on the cold metal roof, grounding herself in its stillness. The morning air smelled faintly of salt and damp pine. A gull cried overhead, distant and lonely, and the branches stirred like the town itself was exhaling in slow motion. It should have been calming. It only sharpened the quiet.

Ryan's words kept replaying back through her thoughts, playing on a loop she couldn't cut loose. There had been a rawness in him, a flash of something unguarded she hadn't expected. It made her want to trust him. That want felt reckless.

Trust was a luxury she couldn't afford, not now. Not with someone out there circling their streets and too many lies still buried under the surface.

Was he standing close to the fire, or feeding it? She hated how easily her heart leaned toward the first answer when her instincts whispered the second. He stood where all the broken pieces seemed to meet, and she could no longer tell if he was trying to hold them together or learning which ones would crack first.

If Ryan was using her, if he was weaving her into something she could not yet see, she wasn't sure she would survive what that would do to her.

She slid into the driver's seat and gripped the steering wheel until her hands ached. The air inside the car felt close, pressing in as though the walls of this town had followed her there. Somewhere in Havenport, the truth was hiding in the corners.

Just as she pulled away from the café, Lena sped past on her bike. Claire caught her eye through the windshield and gave a small nod, part caution and part recognition. Lena dipped her head in return, unsure whether the warning was meant for her or if Claire was caught in her own storm.

Lena pressed forward, legs working harder against the chill in the air. The usual ease of her ride felt distant. Her breath came in clouds. Her thoughts scattered as the familiar roads blurred around her. Even now, she tried to tell herself this was normal. Another training ride, another morning.

But it wasn't.

The whispers about the Ghost Rider hadn't stopped. Every

time she rounded a bend or coasted downhill, her body tensed, waiting for a sound that wasn't there, a flash of movement just behind her.

The town itself felt thinner lately, like the silence between houses was listening. She thought of the upcoming Classic. She'd spent months preparing. Every hill, every long ride in the dark, every early morning had built toward this race. But lately, even that dream felt stained.

A tight curve loomed ahead, slick with wet leaves. Her front wheel skidded just enough to jolt her balance, and her heart slammed hard against her ribs. She caught herself and clipped back in, forcing her legs to keep moving.

She slowed her pace, doubt sinking in for the first time. What if it's not worth it anymore? What if riding makes me a target? The thought was foreign. She'd never questioned cycling before.

The fear was harder to shake now. She had wanted the crown, the glory, and the win; the proof she belonged in the front. But the crown came with eyes on her back. With silence that trailed her wheels.

Still, she couldn't stop. Not yet. Not when she'd worked so hard. Not when the road was still the only place she felt like herself.

A memory flashed: riding along the cliffs last spring, laughing as the wind whipped through her hair. She had flown across the pavement that day, wheels humming in perfect rhythm, the world shrinking to nothing but breath and speed. That wild, unstoppable joy had felt eternal, like the roads were hers alone and would always be.

Now it felt distant, like a story she had once lived but could no longer reach. The cliffs in her memory were bright and open; the cliffs in her mind now were dark, heavy with the eyes she could not see. She tried to summon that same reckless laughter, but all she found was the tight coil in her chest that never seemed to loosen anymore.

She used to chase the wind. Now she rode as if the wind were chasing her.

As she was nearing her neighborhood, she found herself glancing back. Not once, but twice. A chill rippled up her spine. The street behind her was empty, but her hand still rested on the brake, ready.

She turned the corner and saw her house. Modest, tranquil, and hers. She rolled up the driveway and dismounted. Her fingers trembled slightly as she locked up her bike. She checked the latch twice. Then again.

Inside, the door clicked shut behind her, and the silence took over. The air was warmer here. She leaned against the door for a long moment, the breath she'd been holding finally released.
    She was safe, for now.

But the quiet didn't soothe her the way it should have. It

pressed close, like the house was listening. The rhythm of her ride still pulsed faintly in her legs, a ghost of motion that refused to leave her body.

Her gaze drifted across the small, familiar space. The framed race photos, the polished helmet on the counter, the medals lined neatly along the shelf; proof of everything she'd built, every mile that had carried her. They used to make her feel strong. Now they feel like a target.

She ran a hand through her damp hair, the strands trembling faintly between her fingers. Being the best had once felt like armor. Now it felt like a crown she couldn't take off, gleaming just enough to catch the wrong kind of eyes.

She turned away from the shelf and sank onto the edge of the couch. For the first time, the road hadn't followed her home in triumph. It had followed her home in silence, curling into the corners of her small living room like mist that refused to lift.

Across town, that same quiet was spreading, settling over Havenport as though the whole community paused, mid-breath.

Liam was hunched over his laptop in his small office. His desk was cluttered with hastily scrawled notes, scattered newspaper clippings, and a few printed photographs he'd been poring over for days.

He took a sip of now-cold coffee, grimacing as he set the mug down. The article was shaping up to be more than a simple report. It wasn't mere speculation. It was a sharp mix of facts and raw truth, rooted in long-buried secrets.

Starting with the basics, he typed carefully, painting a picture of the victims that emphasized their humanity and place in the story. Each name on the list seemed larger than the last, a progression of broken lives.

He paused, recalling his conversations from earlier that day at Millie's and the community center. Fear and anger. Theories laced with panic and superstition. His job was to reflect the mood without inflaming it further.

Switching tactics, he began weaving a timeline, tying each attack to the whispers and warnings that had followed. The broken spoke had appeared at every scene. It meant something.

What was the message? He drummed his fingers, rereading what he'd typed. The phrase "Ghost Rider" appeared again and again. A myth at first, but myths didn't leave bodies in their wake.

He remembered Erin's voice at Millie's, low and nervous: "Do you think it's a ritual? A cycle?"

And Nessa. Her words stuck more stubbornly than he expected. Her contempt for cyclists. Her unease. Her presence at the edge of things.

As dusk cooled the edges of the sky, Liam sat back. This wasn't just another story. It was personal; his chance to make sense of the chaos for the people who were living through it.

His fingers hovered over the keys again. Jacob Whitley wasn't just a name. He'd been a fixture at the café, a steady presence on the roads. His death wasn't background noise. It was a signal.

He wrote:
Each cyclist's murder strikes deeper, not just into the heart of a community, but into its belief in safety. This isn't random. Each victim was known and valued. Each one has gone.

He stared at the line, then added in the margin: *Each carried something the others leaned on. Control. Bravado. Light. Rhythm. Comfort.*

It looked like the shape of something, a structure being dismantled, one pillar at a time.

The room was quiet enough that he could hear the hum of the old fluorescent light and the faint tap of branches against the window. Havenport itself seemed to be holding its breath.

He turned back to his notes: The Ghost Rider. The spoke. The fear.

He tapped in a few lines from Erin's conversation:
"It's a message," she said. "It's saying, you can't escape this."

He moved to Nessa's quotes and the way she'd said them.

"People think they're invincible on those damn bikes," she muttered. "Shadows catch up to everyone sooner or later."

"Not everyone rides forever. Some of us get off before it takes something from us."

It had sounded bitter then, but now it read more like a confession. He underlined it in his notes and read it again. Her resentment wasn't just about cyclists. It was personal. Maybe even rooted in pain.

He added context sparingly, letting her words carry. The more he reread them, the more he realized what Erin had guessed might be true. Nessa wasn't just a bystander. She was a fracture line.

Liam sat back, the room now wrapped in silence. What he had on screen wasn't just a draft. It was a warning. He had a choice. Stay above the surface, or keep digging, even if it took him places he didn't want to go.

He glanced once more at Nessa's quotes. Saved the file. The screen dimmed, casting back only his reflection.

Even the darkest things leave tracks. You just have to know where to look.

10

A Wild Card in Play

The morning draped itself in muted tones, the streets hushed and subdued. A stillness that blurred and softened judgment. An atmosphere made for someone like Nessa Greene.

Detective Sandoval stepped into the haze, fatigue pressing down on her. The early hour didn't bother her as much as the feeling that lingered. She was used to restlessness, to dreams interrupted by fragments of unsolved cases. But this morning, it wasn't just exhaustion. It was the sense that something unseen had been here first.

Outside the café, a row of abandoned bikes leaned haphazardly. Nessa stood near them, still as stone, her gaze fixed somewhere past the edge of sight. As Claire approached, a chill threaded through her ribs. Nessa's presence had become almost routine, but her timing always felt off, like she arrived before the moment decided to happen.

"Nessa," Claire said, tone flat but cordial. "What brings you here?"

Nessa turned slowly, eyes unfocused. "The fog," she murmured. "It carries whispers today."

Claire frowned. "Whispers don't solve murders. You here to stir things up again, or do you have something useful to say?"

A faint smile. "Useful is a matter of timing."

"Then clarify."

"Clarify?" Nessa echoed, like testing the shape of the word. "You chase answers as if they stay still long enough to catch. They don't. Not here."

Claire's voice tightened. "Are you saying you know who's behind this?"

"I'm saying the roads remember what people forget," Nessa said softly. "The way the wind bends around certain names. The way the ground holds where they fell."

Claire hesitated. "You talk like you've seen this before."

Nessa's eyes flicked toward the tree line. "I mapped those trails once. Long ago. Before the race had fences or finish lines. Every rise, every hollow. The roads don't forget their first shape."

Claire's breath caught, though she didn't know why. "Mapped

them?"

Nessa tilted her head. "Someone had to listen while they were still speaking."

Before Claire could press further, a familiar voice cut through the stillness.

"Claire. Nessa."

Liam strolled up, his usual calm edged with curiosity, notebook tucked loosely in one hand. "Morning chat, or something more?"

Nessa turned toward him, her mood shifting like a change in light. "Always in the right place, Liam," she teased. "I was offering the detective a little perspective."

Liam raised a brow. "On the murders?"

"Or the dark," Nessa replied. "Sometimes they're the same thing."

Claire snapped, her patience thinning. "Enough riddles. If you've got something real, say it."

Nessa's eyes shifted toward her, unreadable. She stepped a fraction closer, voice lowering. "The killer knows these streets like a lover. When to push, wait, and when to strike. It's not instinct. It's intimate."

Liam's posture shifted, his curiosity sparking. "Sounds like you know more than you're admitting."

Nessa's smile vanished. "Let's just say I'm familiar with the dark."

The words hung between them. For a moment, even the hum of passing traffic seemed to recede.

Claire's jaw tightened. "What is it with you and these murders, Nessa? Why are you so invested?"

"Maybe I want to understand," she said softly. "Or maybe I want someone to understand me."

Liam studied her, head tilted slightly. "You've been showing up a lot lately. Almost like you're watching for something."

"Maybe I am," she said. Her gaze slid past both of them, toward the fog thinning over the square. "Maybe we all are."

She turned before either of them could speak again, walking straight ahead with the eerie stillness of someone who already knew where the road beneath her feet would end.

Claire watched her go, unsettled by how the square seemed to bend around her absence. "She knows more than she says."

Liam's gaze stayed locked on Nessa's fading silhouette. "She's not the only one hiding something. Havenport has a lot of masks, and we've only peeled back the first layer."

Claire crossed her arms. "Masks crack eventually."

"Or people forget which face is theirs," Liam said quietly. His voice had lost its usual easy tone.

Nessa's boots struck the cobblestones, like she was keeping time only she could hear. She never once looked back.

Claire glanced at Liam, noticing how closely he tracked Nessa's every step. He had been echoing her instincts more often lately, trusting her judgment without question. It should have been reassuring.

Instead, it felt like standing on thin ice. She wasn't sure what unnerved her more: that he was starting to trust her judgment completely, or that she might be wrong.

At the edge of the square, Nessa paused. She didn't break stride, but her shoulders lifted, as if she could feel their eyes still on her. Then she smiled at herself and walked down a side street.

Just beyond her shoulder, neon cut across the square. Ryan. His bike carved a clean line before spilling onto the open road. Nessa's head lifted just slightly as he passed. Then, she was gone.

Ryan rose from the seat as the street dipped, legs steady against the pull of the hill. The noise from the square faded behind him until only the sound of his tires and the thud of his heartbeat remained.

He wasn't riding for speed. He rode to quiet the noise in his head.

The ridge loop curved out toward the quarry and back again. He had been riding it since he was a teenager, back when the roads felt endless. The air smelled faintly of pine and salt, sharp where the wind pushed off the water. His body moved on instinct, like the bike had grown used to him.

For a while, it almost felt like the old days. But it never lasted. A prickle crept across the back of his neck, the same feeling that had followed him for weeks. Like something was pacing him just out of sight. He glanced back.

It was never just him on these roads anymore. Every turn felt borrowed. Every climb felt like it had belonged to someone else, first. He could almost sense them in the quiet. Not voices, just the shape of their absence close behind his wheels, waiting to see if he would falter.

His breath came fast. He steadied it, two counts in, two out, until the fire in his legs sharpened. He climbed standing, balanced, rocking the bike side to side in the smooth sway he'd taught a hundred times. It looked effortless. It didn't feel like an effort at all.

He wondered if this was what they had felt just before they were gone, that strange calm when your body moves perfectly, but your mind still knows something is wrong. The thought flashed before he could stop it. Maybe he didn't belong on these roads anymore. Or maybe they belonged to him now, in ways no one else could see.

The final climb eased, giving way to the long stretch back to town. He lowered into it, body close to the bars, letting the speed carry him. When the rooftops appeared, he softened his grip, letting the pace ease.

As he rolled past the station, no one looked up from the steps. A breeze cut across the street and rattled a paper on the door. Ryan coasted by without slowing, looking straight ahead, as if he'd never been there at all.

The air inside the Havenport Police Department felt tighter than it should have, as if the building itself had gone tense.

Chief Monroe stood behind his desk, flipping through reports with more irritation than interest.

He didn't look up as he spoke. "Got a call from the County Commissioner this morning," he said. "They want us to bring in the FBI."

Ben stood near the window, arms crossed, jaw set. He turned slowly. "You're serious."

"I'm dead serious." Monroe finally raised his eyes. Five victims. The community is panicking. The press is circling like vultures. And now the commissioner wants to know why we haven't asked for federal help."

He let the file in his hand drop onto the desk. The sound

cracked the stillness. "You want to take that call?"

Ben pushed away from the window and stepped closer, each movement deliberate. "Claire's closer than anyone thinks. Bringing in outside agents now will set us back. They'll bulldoze the scene, shove the case into a mold it doesn't fit, and we'll lose everything she's built."

Monroe leaned forward, bracing his hands on the desk. "That sounds like speculation. Claire's been chasing fog and theories. Now you're backing her up?"

"It's not fog," Ben said, voice steady. "It's instinct. She's connecting threads that don't show up on paper."

Monroe's stare narrowed. "Is this about her, or is this about you?"

Ben hesitated, just for a second, but enough for Monroe to see the crack.

"I've got skin in this too," he said. "My niece rides those same roads. She trains before class, and she's out there. These victims weren't just random. They were cyclists, like her. Like the whole town."

Monroe's tone dropped to a dangerous calm. "So now you're emotional."

"Damn right I am," Ben shot back. "Because this stopped being clean and procedural four bodies ago. We keep pretending like this is just about evidence and timelines. It's not. It's about someone out there trying to tear this place apart from the inside."

Monroe's silence lingered, heavy. He sank slowly into his chair, studying Ben. "And Claire sees that?"

Ben's jaw tightened. "She sees more than that. She sees the psychology behind it. The escalation, the ritual. She's not just solving a case; she's reading a manifesto written in blood and bike chains."

Monroe's expression changed. "And if what she's seeing isn't real? If she's seeing what she *needs* to see to make sense of it?"

The words landed hard. Ben felt them hit because they had already lived in him; quiet, unspoken, surfacing in moments when Claire's eyes had gone distant and frantic all at once. He had seen the toll it took when guilt and obsession started to braid together.

"She's not unraveling," he said finally. "She's closer than she's ever been. And if she starts to slip, I'll be the first to pull her back."

Monroe watched him for a long moment, then spoke. "You believe in her that much?"

Ben nodded. "Enough to risk my reputation. And enough to admit I was wrong for not listening sooner."

Monroe glanced at the files strewn across his desk, the corner of his mouth tightening. "If we're wrong, and this thing spins further out, the fallout won't just hit her. It'll land on both of you."

Ben's voice went quiet. "I can live with that. I can't live with losing another kid. Especially not one I love."

The words hung there, raw. Monroe's shoulders slumped. He exhaled, long and slow, then leaned back in his chair.

"She gets one more week," he said. "After that, if we don't have something concrete, I'm making the call."

Ben gave a small nod. He left the office without another word, the door clicking shut behind him. The hall outside felt colder. Each step carried more than the last, as though he was walking with the burden of Claire's fight.

Outside, Havenport held its breath. The morning was dull, and the streets were empty. The town moved slowly, unaware it was already unraveling. It was being watched with calm pleasure. Each broken body; each silenced breath. Every fall was placed exactly where it was meant to land. The next piece was already in play.

Lena moved through the world like she was immune to its weight. She rose before the town woke, carving lines across roads that still belonged to shadows. She trained where the pavement split and the trees pressed close, where silence could swallow a scream.

Learning her rhythm and the precise movement of her pedals. The small dip of her shoulder on descents. The way she never glanced back, not once, as if what followed her didn't matter. She believed that strength was enough to keep her untouched and that mastery could outpace what waited in the dark. It couldn't.

What she didn't understand, what none of them did, was that strength didn't protect you. It only marked where to strike. That was why she had to be the one. Her fall would not just end her. It would undo the illusion that anyone was untouchable; that willpower could keep them safe. That victory was proof of survival.

The image was already there: The stunned faces and the split silence. The sudden crack in the town's belief that riding fast enough could keep fear from catching up.

Lena wouldn't just fall. She would break the story they had written about themselves. And when she fell, Havenport would understand. Strength was never safety. It was only bait. She wasn't just the next target. She was the fulcrum.

The final movement that would tip everything. And Havenport wasn't ready. But Lena never saw herself as the center of anything. All she felt were the miles and the weight that came with them.

The house was dark when Lena stepped inside, her cleats clicking once on the tile before she took them off. The sound echoed too sharply in the quiet. The air smelled faintly of chain lube and laundry soap, like it always did after training days, sharp and sterile.

She moved through the hall without turning on the lights. The framed race photos on the wall caught slivers of moonlight, glossy smiles frozen mid-victory. They watched her as she passed, or maybe she only imagined they did.

Her muscles pulsed with leftover adrenaline, not strength, just static buzzing through tired bones. The ache was deep enough to hollow her out.

Upstairs, she meant to head for the shower, but her body turned toward her bedroom instead.

Her room was still warm from the day. A faint hum from the mini fan filled the silence. Sweat dried cold on her skin as she crossed to her desk.

She pulled open the bottom drawer and slid out the thin red scrapbook she hadn't touched in years. It felt lighter than she remembered, like it might disintegrate if she held it too tightly. Construction paper pages curled at the corners, the binding tape worn soft.

She carried it to her bed and sat cross-legged, legs trembling faintly. The first page stopped her. Ten-year-old Lena, caked in mud, laughing like the wind was hers. A crooked ribbon dangled from her handlebars. The photo edges were creased from years of eager fingers.

She remembered the smell of that day: sun on wet dirt, the

faint burn of brake pads, and her father's voice tearing through the air as she flew past the finish line. The memory hurt in a way that had nothing to do with pain. Her thumb traced the girl's mud-smeared grin. That girl hadn't calculated. She hadn't measured cadence or heart rate. She had ridden until her lungs burned and then begged for one more lap.

Page after page whispered under her fingertips; races, medals, podiums, grins that grew straighter, stiffer, more careful. Each one glimmered and felt just as breakable. The joy had sharpened into something brittle without her noticing.

She stopped at a newspaper clipping tucked near the back: *Local Prodigy Dominates Regional Classic.* The headline had felt like a crown the day it ran. Now it just felt heavy.

Lena closed the book gently, palms pressing the soft-worn cover. The hum of the fan seemed suddenly too loud. Everyone thought she chased victory. But the truth was simpler and lonelier. She didn't ride to win. She rode because stopping meant finding out who she was without it.

The drawer slid shut with a thud. For a long moment, she sat still. Her breathing slowed, but her pulse didn't. Almost by instinct, she stood. Her hands were already reaching for tomorrow's gear, as though her body had decided before her mind caught up.

At the window, a sound reached her; faint, distant, and metallic. A bell. It carried once through the night air, then vanished. Her chest went still. She stayed there until the silence settled again, heavy and complete.

Lena turned off the light, and the room dissolved into darkness, leaving only the empty road waiting for morning.

11

The Edge of Trust

Ryan Moore's breath clouded in the cold air as he hesitated outside Haven Cycle Repair. He hadn't seen Marissa in a long time; not since his last attempt to reconnect had been met with silence and a look that chilled him more than winter ever had.

He pushed the door open. The familiar scent of oil and rubber wrapped around him. Marissa stood at her workbench, back to the door, shoulders tight. Her eyes were fixed on a partially disassembled bike frame.

"Marissa," Ryan said, louder than he intended.

She stilled. For a long second, she didn't turn. When she did, her expression changed, surprised, then something that looked like fear. It vanished quickly, replaced by a blank stare.

"Ryan," she said flatly. "Didn't expect you."

He closed the door behind him. "We need to talk."

She looked back at the frame, but he noticed how her hand tightened around the wrench. "We said everything last time."

"The murders," he said. "They're escalating. And I keep coming back to you."

She laughed. "So, I'm a suspect now? Because I don't show up at races? Because I keep to myself?"

"Because something's different," he said. "Not just since the accident. Before that, you were still you. Fierce and brilliant. Now it's like you're watching the world burn."

Marissa slowly set the wrench down. "You think you know what it's like to have everything taken from you? To watch the life you built get erased, piece by piece?"

"I don't," Ryan admitted. "That's why I'm here. To try. Because of the way you're acting. It's like you've already decided who you need to be to survive. And I'm not sure that person would stop short of anything."

Her gaze met his, and for a moment, the unease shifted. "You're not here for answers. You're here for absolution."

"What does that mean?"

"You want me to say I didn't do it. So, you can feel better about walking away again."

"I don't want to walk away," he said.

"But you will."

They stood in silence. The hum of a distant space heater filled the room like static.

Then Marissa spoke, her voice softer now. "The old Marissa is gone, Ryan. She died on that road. Every part of her that believed in second chances, in fair races, in being seen... gone."

"There's still a part of you that cares," he said. "I saw it just now. When I walked in."

"No," she said, and for once, she didn't sound angry. Just tired. "You saw what you wanted to see."

Ryan stepped closer. "Tell me you had nothing to do with it. Look me in the eye and say it."

Her jaw clenched, but her expression didn't change. "I'm not your villain, Ryan. But I'm not your redemption either."

Something fractured in him. Not broken but cracked. "You said people underestimate you. I don't."

"Yes," she said softly. "You do. Because you still think I'm looking for forgiveness."

He stared at her, searching for the girl he used to know. But all he saw was a stranger wearing her face.

"I guess I have no choice," he murmured and left.

Outside, the cold hit harder. He zipped his jacket up to his chin, but the chill that gripped his chest wasn't weather. It was regret, and something else.

His boots trudged along the narrow pavement. The town stirred; early traffic, clinking dishes behind shuttered windows. Familiar sounds. But none of it felt right.

He kept thinking about Marissa, how distant she'd become. About the wrench in her hand when he walked in, and the edge in her voice when she said, "You still think I'm looking for forgiveness."

She wasn't. And that terrified him more than anything else. He had told himself he had given her space to heal. That backing off was kindness. But it hadn't been. It had been fear. And now, that fear had a cost.

The café appeared ahead, its windows blurred with condensation, golden light spilling out like a whispered invitation. It looked warm and safe. But even that felt like a lie.

Ryan paused on the edge of the curb, scanning the street. That familiar prickle again. He turned, searching for movement, but the street offered nothing back. His heart thudded once, then relaxed. Just nerves. That's what he told himself. But deep down, he knew better.

He inhaled slowly and stepped forward. He could still turn back. Could still choose to stay out of the deeper layers. But that version of himself, the one who stayed neutral to avoid causing harm, wasn't enough anymore. Protecting people had once meant staying silent. Now he wasn't sure silence protected anyone at all.

He opened the door and stepped into the warmth. The scent of coffee and the soft clink of mugs. Conversations were low and murmured. A few heads turned, then returned to their business. But Claire noticed.

She sat by the window, notebook open, posture composed. That familiar, distant sharpness was there, but it softened the instant she saw him. Not accusing, assessing. Reading him the way she read crime scenes.

Ryan hesitated just inside the door. That old instinct, to observe instead of act, pulled at him. But he ignored it. He crossed the room and slid into the seat across from her. His face was pale, tight with the words he hadn't said.

"Ryan," Claire greeted, looking up. "You look like you've seen a ghost."

He gave a weak smile, ran a hand over his face as if he could wipe the last hour away. "In a way, I have. I just came from Marissa's."

Claire's expression tightened slightly.

"What happened?"

He leaned forward, lowering his voice. "She's changed, Claire.

Not just distant. There's something darker now. Before, I thought it was just bitterness, but... It's like she knows something she's not admitting."

"You think she's involved?"

"I don't want to," Ryan said honestly. "But she doesn't talk like someone trying to clear her name. She talks like someone who's done pretending."

He paused, frowning. "She told me people only see what she lets them see. It felt like a warning. Like she was daring me to look deeper."

Claire absorbed that in silence.

"You think she's playing a game?" she asked finally.

Ryan nodded. "I think she's always played one. But now it's different. It's more... personal."

For a moment, neither of them spoke. The café around them moved softly, untouched by the friction at their table. Claire's fingers drummed once on the table, then stopped.

"I need to see her myself," she said.

Ryan reached across the table and rested his hand on hers. It wasn't affection, it was concern. "Be careful. She's good at hiding what's real. She's always been good at that."

Claire's expression softened. "I know. But I need to see it for myself. I can't base this on your instincts alone."

He pulled back slowly, his face marked by a soft ache. "Don't let her twist it. She's sharp, and she knows how to make people second-guess what they know."

"I've dealt with worse," Claire replied. But the way her voice dipped suggested she wasn't as certain as she wanted to be.

Ryan didn't push. "I hope I'm wrong," he said.

"So do I," Claire whispered, gathering her coat.

She stepped out into the town again. The streets were hushed, the day folding into itself. She drove with intention. Each turn familiar, but heavy now. As she pulled up to Haven Cycle, the dull neon sign buzzed faintly.

Claire shifted the car into park and looked in the mirror. Her eyes met her own, sharp but uncertain. Ryan's voice replayed in her mind.

Be careful. She's a master at hiding what's going on inside.

Claire opened the door and stepped out. Gravel crunched underfoot. The bell over the door jangled as she entered. Marissa was at her workbench. The glow of a small desk lamp cast long lines across her face. She didn't flinch. She kept her head low, meeting the moment as if she had been expecting it.

"Detective Sandoval," she said without looking up. "What brings you here?"

Claire stepped inside, the door clicking shut behind her. The shop was silent, but not lifeless. It felt suspended. Half-assembled bikes and scattered parts hinted at work in progress or maybe work left undone.

"I wanted to speak with you directly," Claire said. Her steps were calm and deliberate. "Thought it was time for a real conversation."

Marissa turned. The warmth Claire had seen in old photos was gone. What remained was worn and guarded.

"Let me guess. Ryan sent you."

Claire shook her head. "This was my call. I needed to see you for myself."

Marissa's lips curled faintly. "So, what do you expect to find here, Detective? A confession? A missing piece of evidence? Or just a woman you've already decided is broken?"

"I don't know what I'll find," Claire said. "But I know you've been holding back."

Marissa folded her arms. "Everyone is. You included."

Claire didn't respond right away. "Then maybe it's time we stop pretending otherwise."

Marissa's expression darkened. "Ryan doesn't understand what it's like to lose everything. He still sees me as who I was."

Claire studied her face. "I see someone who's still connected to this community, even if it's from the outside. You're still here. Still in it. Why?"

Marissa looked away for a moment, then back at Claire. "Because this is the last thing I have that still feels real. The bikes, the work, and the road."

Claire felt a tug she didn't expect. Not sympathy, more recognition. She had spent enough time on the fringes of her own life to know the look of someone trying not to disappear.

"It's not my job to pity you," Claire said. "But I am trying to understand you."

"Why?" Marissa asked, voice tense. "Because you think I'm involved?"

"I think you've seen more than you're admitting," Claire replied. "And I think your silence is telling me something."

Marissa's shoulders tensed. "You want a motive? Fine. I'm angry. I'm tired. I'm bitter. But that doesn't make me guilty."

"No, it doesn't," Claire said, her voice even. "But it makes me ask more questions."

Marissa looked at her. "You don't trust me."

"I don't have the luxury of trust," Claire said. "I work with facts, and what I see is someone close to this case who hasn't been fully honest."

Marissa turned back to her workbench, her voice lower now. "Then look harder. Because not all truth is neat, and not every wound leaves a clean mark."

Claire paused in silence, then stepped back toward the door.

"I'm not here to judge you," she said. "But I can't ignore you either."

As she pulled the door open, cold air swept back into the shop. Marissa didn't look up.

Claire stepped outside, the sound of the bell fading behind her. As she walked away, she felt it; the unease that came when instinct and evidence didn't line up. She had come in looking for answers. Instead, she had walked into a mirror. And that, more than anything, made her question what she might be missing.

Back inside, Marissa let out a slow breath and reached up to rub her neck. Her fingers traced a scar that had long since faded, though it never disappeared from memory. The rough patch of skin was a reminder; one she tried not to think about too often. One that refused to be forgotten.

What does she want from me? Marissa thought, a mix of frustration and fatigue settling over her. Claire's questions were probing. Marissa had met them with the same guardedness she'd recently adopted.

She knew why the detective was asking about the recent murders, and sensed that Claire was trying to dig deeper, to understand not only the case, but her. Marissa didn't want to be understood. Not anymore.

She turned to the workbench, her fingers trailing absently over the tools laid out in neat rows. Each wrench, each pair of pliers, was a piece of the life she had built after the fall. A life defined by repairs instead of races, by fixing instead of winning. The shift had been slow, inevitable. She had adapted, or at least that's what she told herself on the better days.

She closed her eyes, and the memories came rushing back, vivid and relentless: the accident. The shock slammed into her all over again, as the sickening crunch of metal replayed in her mind.

The road was slick that day, enough to make every turn a gamble. She'd known the risks; she'd always known them. She'd believed in her own invincibility, the way the young and fast can.

The pain had been blinding, radiating from her leg and up her spine. She remembered the taste of blood in her mouth; the sting of gravel embedded in her skin. But most of all, it was the sound that stayed with her. The eerie silence after the fall, the absence of any help. No fellow riders turned. No hands reached out. Just the hollow rush of the wind past her ears. The slow, creeping realization that she was alone on the road.

Her broken body was twisted like the bike that lay beside her.

She clenched her fists, her nails digging into her palms. Time had passed, but the anger burned just as fiercely. Why hadn't they stopped? It was a question that never had an answer, not really. She had heard their laughter as they rode on, catching the distant banter as they moved ahead without a glance. It had been a joke to them, an inconvenience on a long ride.

The anger was always there, beneath the surface, mingling with deeper sadness. It wasn't the accident that haunted her. It was the loss of everything she had been. She wasn't a racer anymore. She was a mechanic. She was someone people came to when they needed a bike fixed, not someone they cheered for at the finish line.

Is this all that's left? The question surfaced, bitter and familiar. A small part of her still longed for the past, even when she knew it was pointless. She understood who she was now. No matter how hard she tried to be content, the truth remained. She missed the races and the wind in her face. The roar in her chest as she surged past someone and remembered what it was like to be unstoppable.

And in the quietest corner of her mind, something darker whispered: maybe they didn't deserve what they had kept when she lost everything.

Marissa let out a shaky breath, suddenly aware of how small the shop was. How suffocating it was. The walls, covered with posters of past cycling events, seemed to lean closer. They were relics of a world she no longer belonged to, a world that had moved on without her. She left them hanging, not because she still believed, but because taking them down would mean admitting defeat.

Who am I kidding? she thought bitterly. The life she'd built here wasn't what she wanted. It was what was left. The races had defined her; they had given her a purpose she hadn't found in anything else. Without them, she had no sense of direction. Floating in the wreckage of a career that had ended too soon.

"You're not that person anymore," she reminded herself. "You're Marissa, the mechanic."

The words rang hollow, fading into the stillness of the empty shop. She stared at her hands, roughened by the work that was never meant to be hers. Strong and precise. The kind that could break something just as easily as fix it.

Her gaze drifted to the row of bikes lined against the wall. Each one repaired under her watchful eye, each one made whole again while she stayed fractured. She wondered, not for the first time, what it might feel like to do the opposite; to take something perfect and make it unrideable. The thought came and went in a flicker, fast enough to scare her.

She pushed it away. She had to.

She took one last glance at the old race posters, pausing on a photo of herself, mid-sprint, her face filled with determina-tion. She wondered if that version of her would even recognize the woman she had become, or if she'd be afraid of her. The thought was too sharp to hold, so she turned away, picking up the wrench with trembling hands.

The past wasn't something she could shake. With Claire unearthing old wounds and death clinging to the streets, the darkness didn't just swirl around Marissa. It had moved in. And sometimes, when the shop was quiet and the wind pressed against the windows, she wondered if the darkness had simply been waiting for her all along.

12

Veiled Intentions

Claire sat in her small, cluttered office, the hum of the building faint through the walls. The station felt hollow at this hour, just her and the sharp smell of cold coffee. Case files leaned in slouched piles across the desk, their edges soft from weeks of being handled.

Her laptop screen threw pale light across the sprawl of notes and marked-up printouts. She'd been combing the Gazette archives for hours, chasing gaps, not leads; hoping something would finally break open.

Then her eyes caught on a half-forgotten headline.

Cyclist Killed in Late-Night Accident Near Briar's Peak.
  Liam Harper

Five years ago. A fatal crash on a fog-thick night. Halfway through, her gaze stopped cold on a name she hadn't expected. Nessa Greene. Listed as a witness. One of the only people nearby. Claire blinked hard, then read the sentence again.

Her account had been vague; shadows, fog, nothing clear. The case had gone cold, shelved, forgotten. But Nessa stayed. The thought landed hard in her gut. She sat back, the chair hinge groaning, and stared at the screen.

Claire stood abruptly, pushing the chair back hard enough that it rattled. She crossed the room to her board. The victims stared back from their photos; paper faces flat and pale in the lamplight. The single bagged spoke hung at the center like a pin through all of them. She unhooked it, the metal cold through the plastic.

Victor controlled every variable until he couldn't. Elliot, reckless, always pushing just past the safe line. Megan carried everyone else's hope until it buried her. Derek, methodical to the point of rigidity. Jacob, steady, the one people leaned on until he collapsed.

They weren't random. They were structural. Load-bearing pieces, taken out one by one.

And Ryan... Claire's gaze drifted to his photo in the corner of the board, still unmarked, still whole. He didn't belong there, not really. And yet, he fit too well. That was what unsettled her most. He carried pieces of them all: flashes of certainty, recklessness, hope, order, and quiet strength woven together in a way that shouldn't coexist yet somehow did.

It gave him gravity. People leaned toward Ryan without

realizing it, as if standing close might steady them. She'd felt it too; the subtle pull, the way his voice could cut through her thoughts like a clear line on a chaotic map.

And that terrified her. The same qualities that drew her in were the ones that marked him. If the pattern she'd been chasing was real, he didn't just fit inside it. He anchored it. He was the point where all the broken lines converged, the center of a web that might already be tightening around him.

Her pen hovered over the photo without touching it. Part of her wanted to mark it, to name the danger. Another part wanted to tear it down entirely, to protect it from the pattern clawing at everything else.

Her pulse quickened, and she forced herself to look away. She couldn't let this blur; not now. Yet when she closed her eyes, she didn't see evidence or patterns. She saw the vulnerability that slipped through when he thought no one was watching. The way his voice softened when he said her name.

It made her question everything: her judgment, her instincts, even the clean lines she'd drawn between truth and feeling. If the killer saw Ryan as the keystone, then he wasn't standing on the edge of danger. He was its center.

And if she was wrong about him, if he wasn't a target at all... then maybe he was something far worse. The thought settled over her. Her jaw tightened. This wasn't chaos. It was designed.

Her eyes moved to Lena's photo, still untouched, still standing, for now. Lena's grin seemed alive even on paper, bright and careless, the kind of expression that believed in tomorrow. Claire studied it, searching for fractures and finding none. That, more than anything, unsettled her.

The others had carried more in plain sight; lines of worry around their mouths, shadows tucked behind their eyes. Lena carried nothing but momentum. She was all forward motion, no hesitation, like someone convinced that danger only found you if you slowed down long enough to see it coming.

Claire leaned closer, her breath faint on the photo. If the killer was escalating, Lena was everything they would want: visible, admired, untouchable. A living emblem of what this town still believed in. And symbols, Claire knew, were meant to be broken.

That thought left her cold. She didn't want to see Lena that way. She didn't want to see her at all through the killer's eyes.

She set the spoke back carefully, like it might splinter if she dropped it, and reached for her coat hanging on the back of her chair. She stood still in the dim office, her coat half-slipped on one shoulder. The board loomed behind her, every photo holding its breath.

She had been trying to read the pattern forward, but the answer might be buried backward; older than any of the threads she'd been chasing. Her laptop screen still glowed across the desk. She moved back to it, scrolling through the Gazette archive until the headline surfaced again.

The words blurred at first, then sharpened. She read them more slowly this time, letting the space between them speak. No witnesses except a lone passerby, Nessa Greene.

The name seemed to echo louder than it should. Claire tried to picture it. Nessa was on that road before anyone else, the mist swallowing everything but her shape. The report described her statement as vague, almost dreamlike; shadows, silence, nothing certain.

Claire took a photo on her phone and then closed the browser window, the screen going black and showing her reflection in place of the words. Her own face looked distant, fractured by the faint glare of the desk lamp.

If that night was where the first crack appeared, then Nessa had been standing close enough to hear it. And Liam... he had been close enough to write it down. The thought didn't settle like suspicion. It sat like static, an itch she couldn't place.

Claire drew her coat the rest of the way on and flicked off the lamp. The darkness felt cleaner than the light had. It was time to find Liam. If there was something in that old story he hadn't said out loud, she needed to hear it before the pattern claimed anyone else.

Claire made her way to the library, where Liam often worked late into the night. The building was caught in a halo of yellow light from the tall streetlamps. Inside, the scent of old paper and dust filled the air, a comforting presence amidst the growing pressure of the case.

Claire spotted him hunched over a desk, his laptop open and fingers flying across the keyboard. He looked up, surprised to see her.

"Claire," he greeted, closing his laptop. "Didn't expect to see you here this late."

"I've been reading through your old articles," Claire abruptly stated, holding up her phone.

Liam glanced at the screen, then at her. "The accident," he murmured. "That was a rough story to cover."

"Tell me more about it," Claire pressed, sliding into the chair across from him. "What do you remember about Nessa's involvement?"

Liam eased into the seat, running a hand through his tousled hair. "Nessa claimed she was on a late-night walk when it happened. She heard a crash but couldn't see much. When the police arrived, she was standing near the wreck, shaken but coherent. There was nothing to suggest she was the cause."

"Did you believe her?" She pressed.

He paused. "I don't know. Nessa's always been an enigma in this town. She's eccentric, sure. But she's never struck me as violent. Although now that I think of it, there was a strange edge to her that night. She seemed more haunted than scared."

"Haunted by guilt, maybe?" Claire suggested.

"Or worse," Liam countered. "If you're thinking she's behind the recent killings, I'm not convinced. She's unpredictable, but murder? That's a different level of darkness."

A sharp edge crept into Claire's voice. "What about her visions? Do you think she's genuinely seeing things, or is it all part of some twisted game?"

Liam was rigid. "With Nessa, it's hard to tell. I've spent enough time around her to know she believes what she's saying. Whether those visions are real or a manifestation of trauma... I can't say."

Claire considered his words. "I need to talk to her," she said. "I don't trust her... I can't ignore her either."

Liam hesitated. "Be careful, Claire. Nessa isn't predictable. She's... complicated."

Without another word, Claire grabbed her coat and stepped outside, the crisp air biting against her skin. Sliding into her car, she started the engine, the hum breaking the silence.

As she pulled out of the library lot, movement on the opposite sidewalk caught her eye.

A cyclist coasted past, bright jacket flashing in the gray light;

young, maybe twenty. She rode low over the bars, earbuds tucked under her helmet straps. Claire's chest tightened. She braked, rolling her window down as the rider slowed at the crosswalk.

"Hey," Claire called.

The girl turned, startled, then smiled faintly in recognition. Ben's niece; he'd shown Claire photos, proud and a little nervous about her riding the same roads as the victims.

"You should head straight home," Claire said. "No solo rides for a while. Not until we clear this."

The girl's smile faltered. "I thought it would be safe."

"It's not," Claire said, sharper than she meant. She forced her voice down. "Please. ... stay off the back roads for now."

She nodded and pedaled away. Claire watched until she disappeared around the corner. She rolled the window back up, shifted into drive, and pressed on.

Her car crept up the narrow, winding path to Nessa's cabin. The trees flanked the road, their branches intertwining as if closing in around her. The further she went, the colder it became.

Ben would have told her this was reckless. Every instinct said not to go alone. But something about Nessa, the way she appeared like a ghost at every turn, made her believe this had to be one-on-one. Nessa would never open up if she felt cornered.

Arriving at the cabin, Claire hesitated, scanning the tree line. The place felt deliberately isolated, cut off from town life.

This was exactly the kind of place where backup made sense. Still, she climbed the wooden steps, each creak sending a jolt through her nerves, reminding her she was alone.

Nessa answered the door with a hollow look, her pale skin nearly translucent. Her wild hair framed her face, adding to her odd presence.

"Detective Sandoval," she said, her tone flat. "I see curiosity has gotten the best of you."

She held up her phone, displaying the archived article from Liam's report. "I want to talk about the accident you witnessed," she said firmly.

Nessa's green eyes lit up. Whether it was surprise, anger, or amusement, Claire couldn't tell.

"That was years ago," she replied. "A different time. Different ghosts."

"It's still haunting you," Claire pressed, stepping inside the dimly lit cabin. The scent of aged wood and burnt sage clung to the air.

"It's shaping how you see these murders," Claire said carefully. "Or how you want others to see them."

As the door latched behind her, Claire felt the silence close in. Her pulse stayed measured, but her senses sharpened. No radios, just her. She stayed near the edge of the room.

Her eyes swept the space. The latch on the window had been replaced recently. The wood pile beside the stove was neatly stacked. Nessa wasn't chaotic; she was controlled. That alone set Claire's instincts humming.

Scattered artworks lined the walls, charcoal drawings of cyclists. Twisted roads and dark, looming forests appeared repeatedly. Claire paused at one, its rider drawn without a face. It felt less like art and more like evidence. A shiver climbed Claire's spine.

"You don't like cyclists, do you, Nessa?" Claire asked, her tone probing. "Even your artwork shows it."

Nessa's lips curled into a bitter smile. "Cyclists," she repeated, the word dripping with sarcasm. "They ride through this town like it's theirs to conquer. Arrogant, invincible, always chasing glory. They think they own these roads."

"Why such hatred?" Claire asked. "Is it because of the accident?"

Nessa's expression darkened, her eyes drifting to a drawing of a lone cyclist. "Maybe," she shrugged. "I've seen too many of them ignore the warnings, the dangers. It's like they're daring death, and when it comes, they act surprised."

Claire stayed still, weight balanced, ready if she needed to move fast. She watched the small changes, Nessa's tightening jaw, the way her hands stayed still when her words didn't. No defensive startle, no grief, just that simmering control.

"You sound almost... pleased," Claire observed cautiously.

Nessa's face hardened. "I'm not pleased," she snapped. "I'm frustrated. They never learn, never understand the risk they bring to these roads. Their deaths... It's not tragedy, it's inevitability."

"Are you suggesting they deserve this?" Claire asked.

A sudden intensity lit Nessa's face. "Deserve? No. I won't deny there's a certain justice to it. They've always underestimated the dangers here. Now the dangers have found them."

"Or maybe the dangers have found them because of someone like you," Claire countered. "Someone who sees cyclists as a nuisance."

Nessa leaned closer, her voice dropping to a near-whisper. "You think I'm the one doing this? That I'm the one stalking them?"

Her laughter was low and unsettling. "Maybe I'm just watching and listening to the wind."

Claire's eyes didn't leave her. No flinch at the accusation, no denial. Just amusement. That was almost worse.

"And what has it told you?" Claire demanded, her patience wearing thin.

Nessa shifted. "It tells me they'll keep coming, no matter what happens. It tells me the roads will always be hungry."

A wave of frustration and fear rose in Claire. One thing was clear: Nessa's disdain for cyclists was not an abstract feeling. It was deeply personal, primal.

"Why do you stay here, Nessa?" Claire asked, changing tactics. "In this town, among the very people you despise?"

Her face shifted, cool and calculating. "Because Havenport is mine, too. It's not just for them. It's for the ones who see the truth."

Claire noted the phrasing, tucked it away. The ones who see the truth. It wasn't something most people said unless they needed to place themselves apart from the world.

She stepped back, her mind whirling with possibilities. Nessa's words were cryptic; there was a twisted logic to them, one that could easily cross into darker territory.

"If you know what's behind this," Claire urged one last time, "anything that could stop it, you need to say it now."

Nessa's face twisted into a cruel smile. "I've told you enough. The rest… you'll have to find yourself."

Claire left the cabin, her steps quickening the moment the door shut behind her. The air outside hit her like she was surfacing from deep water. No safety net, just instinct and the echo of Nessa's voice in her head. It was clearer than ever: Nessa was hiding something. The only question was whether it was someone else's guilt or her own.

As Claire's footsteps faded down the path, Nessa closed the door and locked it with a deliberate click. The silence in the cabin rushed back like a tide, pressing close around her ribs. She lit another cigarette from the dying ember of the last, the paper crackling as it caught. Smoke curled upward, dissolving into the air.

She sank into her armchair by the window. Her gaze drifted to the small table beside her chair.

There, in a tarnished silver frame, sat the photograph she could never bring herself to put away.

Nessa reached for it, fingertips brushing over the cold glass. It showed a younger version of herself, arm slung around another girl whose grin was all sunlight and wild freedom. Dust streaked their skin, road-tangled hair clung to their faces, but their eyes burned bright with the joy found only on long rides, when the world feels endless and nothing can break you.

Nessa's thumb hovered over her friend's face, her expression softening, then hardening again.

"You were the brave one," she whispered. The words barely stirred the air.

That day had ended with scraped knees, laughter, and a promise to never stop. A promise that had shattered long before the photograph began to fade.

She stubbed her cigarette into the ashtray, grinding it down until only gray ash remained. The sound was sharp in the stillness. The bitterness rose in her chest. She saw them in her mind; cyclists gliding down the roads, oblivious, untouchable, their bright gear slicing through the mist. Pretending they owned it. Assuming the roads would forgive them.

Outside, the trees pressed closer against the window. She could see the faint outline of the old trails, winding like scars through the undergrowth. They were roads she had once loved. Every bend carried a memory she would rather forget.

"They never understood," she muttered. The flame from her lighter flared as she lit another cigarette, painting her features in brief orange light.

"Not until it's too late."

Her eyes returned to the photograph. She studied it as if it were a map of her past. The woman beside her in the picture felt distant now, a name caught on the edge of memory. Time had frayed the line between what had been lost and what might still be out there, waiting.

Nessa drew in a slow breath, letting the smoke sear her lungs before she exhaled. Her voice was quiet, flat. "They never learn."

IV

The Darkening Trail

13

Hidden Connections

As dawn broke, Lena Crawford moved through her pre-ride routine in the narrow entryway of her home. Every detail was in place, gear lined up, and the surfaces clean. But beneath the order, dread tightened in her chest.

Her cycling clothes were folded on the bench by the door. She pulled on her jacket and flexed her fingers inside the gloves. She adjusted the chin strap twice, tugging harder than necessary, as if it could guard her from more than just a fall.

Safety had always come naturally. Lately, it has become a shield. A kind of armor against whatever waited. With each piece of gear she secured, her heartbeat steadied. Her breath came easier. This wasn't fear, it was control. Her way of saying she wouldn't be chased off these roads.

She moved towards the bike, leaning against the door. Her hand ran along the smooth frame, catching the quiet tension in the wheels. This wasn't just a ride. It was how she cleared the static from her mind. These roads, no matter what had happened on them, still belonged to her.

Megan's face flashed in her mind. She had been the one who pushed Lena into the cycling world. She challenged her to ride farther, harder, faster. Lena could still hear her laugh; the kind that made the hardest climbs feel lighter. That laugh felt distant now. The memory stung, not because it was gone, but because it reminded her how fragile everything really was.

Lena clipped her phone into her armband, checked the tire pressure, and tightened her shoes with practiced movements. Then she mounted her bike and pushed off.

She tried to shake off the dread in her chest and concentrated on the road ahead. The Ghost Rider was just a rumor; a story passed between riders. As the trees closed in, the air shifted. A small movement caught her attention. She flinched.

Her fingers clenched the handlebars. Just a branch, swaying in the wind. She made herself let go. *Breathe.* The speed picked up as she reached the main road. Cold air burned her lungs, but it felt good. It reminded her that her body was strong, that she wasn't fragile.

She passed familiar landmarks, places she had trained a hundred times. But this morning, every curve felt like a question. Was she tempting fate? Was the Classic worth the risk? She told herself yes. That riding was a form of defiance. But the further she pedaled from her house, the more that confidence slipped.

At the crest of a familiar hill, the road opened into a clearing above the quarry. She wasn't planning to stop. But something made her slow, a tug in her chest she couldn't ignore.

Then she saw it. A bike was leaning awkwardly against the guardrail just ahead. Black frame, sleek. New. But there was no rider. No one was walking nearby; no parked car, just the bike.

Her breath came faster now. Her hands trembled slightly on the bars. She scanned the trees, and there was nothing, not even birdsong. She stopped, dismounted slowly, every movement deliberate.

"Hello?" she called out.

No answer.

She stepped closer to the guardrail, still scanning. It could be nothing, someone gone to relieve themselves, a jogger returning, or a misread moment. But instinct said otherwise.

She looked down, heart hammering. There was movement below. For a second, all she saw was the glassy surface of the pond, a ripple, and then an arm. Someone was swimming.

Lena leaned forward, bracing a hand on the metal railing. A lone swimmer moved through the dark surface with long, confident strokes. No splashing; no urgency. Just the calm movements of someone fully in control.

The panic in her chest loosened. Not gone but changed. It was strange to see someone choosing to swim here. But nothing was menacing about it. Simply a human refusing to be afraid.

She stood there a moment longer, breathing in the cold morning air, letting it settle her. Then she turned back to her bike and swung one leg over the frame. She pushed off slowly, letting the wheels turn beneath her.

As she headed back to town, the golden light of the Haven Café caught her attention. A familiar car pulled out, and she recognized Sergeant Foster behind the wheel. Ben gave a firm, almost warning nod. The exchange relaxed something inside her; a reminder that someone cared enough to see this through.

By the time she reached her driveway, her legs were burning, and her breath came in measured bursts. She dismounted, bracing herself as she swept the tree line. The road was still, but it didn't feel empty.

Lena unclipped her helmet and paused for a moment before stepping inside. The warmth of her home engulfed her, but the relief was fleeting and shallow. She set her bike against the wall and paused.

She was safe for now.

Across town, Claire stood in her own small kitchen, her body resting against the counter. The ceramic coffee mug was cold, forgotten. Each broken spoke left at the scenes felt like a hushed accusation; another reminder she hadn't stopped this.

She picked up her phone, its screen glowing faintly in the half-light. The message was short, but it burned.

Ryan Moore has been meeting with someone. Same place. Same time. Every Thursday.

Claire reread it, the words stinging with certainty. Same place. Same time. A secret kept from her. She hated how personal it felt. Like she had been naive about letting her guard down. A dangerous mix of anger and disappointment twisted in her chest.

Her mind replayed their recent conversations, the way Ryan's eyes softened when they met hers, his voice dropping just enough to make her listen. He was careful, too careful, steering conversations away from his past. It was subtle, but she noticed.

Claire set the mug down and stared out the window. *What are you hiding, Ryan?*

She didn't want to cross this line, didn't want to taint whatever trust they had built with suspicion. But with another cyclist's life on the line, personal feelings were a luxury she couldn't afford.

She grabbed her coat, fingers trembling as she zipped it. At the door, she hesitated, then picked up her phone again. She stepped outside as it began to ring.

The drive was short but suffocating, the light cut across cracked pavement as she parked near an abandoned garage on the edge of town. It was weathered and grim, the windows streaked with grime, metal shutters groaning when the wind hit them. She knew, even before she spotted Ryan's car, that he was inside.

Claire waited, fixed on the garage. When the door creaked open, her pulse jumped. Ryan stepped out first, his expression tight. An older man followed. Broad-shouldered, silver-streaked hair, and his face was lined with grief.

Dean Harris. Claire remembered him from Elliot's funeral. He hadn't said a word then, hadn't stayed long. Now, here he was, meeting Ryan in secret.

Claire approached. "Dean. I didn't know you were still in Havenport."

"I'm not," he said, his tone flat but unflinching. "I came for this." He glanced toward Ryan, as if the explanation lay with him.

"Every Thursday?" she asked, shifting between them.

Dean didn't flinch. "I wanted answers." He lifted a folder from under his arm. "Ryan offered to help."

Ryan exhaled. His voice was rougher than usual. "You already know why we're here, Claire."

"You've both been keeping secrets," she replied, not as an accusation, but as a truth she couldn't ignore.

Dean's voice dropped. "It was my choice. I asked him not to tell anyone."

Claire studied them both. "Then talk."

The three of them moved to the concrete steps. Dean sat heavily, his hands moving carefully as he opened the folder. Inside were photos, Elliot grinning with his bike, race registrations, scraps of notes. Nothing new in terms of evidence, but everything about it felt personal and raw.

"He was young," Dean said, fixed on one photo. "Too young for everything that came for him."

Claire let the silence hold. She knew grief well enough to let it speak when words couldn't.

Dean's voice was lower now, uneven. "First junior championship at thirteen. They called him fearless. His coaches said he was reckless, but they didn't know him. He rode like he had something chasing him. I thought he just wanted to win."

His jaw tightened. "Now I think he was running from something. He never told me what, and I didn't ask. That's the part I can't forget."

Ryan shifted beside him, looking down at the photos like he was seeing them for the first time.

Claire's attention stayed on Dean. "He wasn't reckless the night he died," she said.

Dean looked at her, his voice sharp and certain. "No. It wasn't an accident. We buried him knowing it was murder. I didn't need a police report to tell me that."

Claire gave a single nod. "What do you want from this, Dean?"

"I want to understand why," he said, his voice cracking. He gestured to Ryan. "He thinks there's a pattern."

"There is," Claire said. "We're following it."

Dean's expression hardened. "Then follow it faster."

The silence returned.

Ryan finally spoke. "I helped him because I needed answers too. You know that."

"I knew you were holding back. I just didn't know if it was about the case, or something else."

Ryan's voice was low. "Maybe both."

Dean closed the folder carefully and handed it to Claire. "This is all I have. I won't be back here again."

Thank you," Claire said softly. "I am so sorry about Elliot."

Dean didn't respond right away, but he didn't look away either.

"I can't change what happened," she added, "but I'll do everything I can to find the truth."

He gave her a single nod before walking away. His steps were slow and heavy, the shape of his grief trailing behind him.

Ryan remained, watching Claire. "You still don't trust me."

"Trust isn't the point," she said. "But I believe you want this solved."

"I do."

"You should have told me," She added.

"I should have," he admitted.

As Claire walked back to her car, each step was marked by the unanswered questions. The folder under her arm felt light, but the truth inside was heavier than anything she'd carried before.

Claire couldn't turn back now. Not when she was this close. She drove through the streets, her hands gripping the wheel too tightly, her mind fixed on the answers she needed.

She pulled up to the curb in front of Ben's apartment. The street was still. Ben was waiting under a streetlamp. He climbed into the car, the sudden warmth cutting through the chill.

"Claire," he said, settling into the seat. His face looked drawn and tired.

"Hey, Ben," Claire replied. "Another long one."

Ben leaned back, rubbing his jaw. "I spoke to Monroe today. He's ready to call the FBI if we don't get results this week. He's feeling pressure from above."

Claire's head snapped towards him. "What did you tell him?"

"That pulling you off this case would be a mistake. You're closer than anyone, and he knows it," Ben said. "I bought you time. But we need to deliver something. Soon."

The words landed hard between them.

Claire's thoughts moved to the broken spokes, the victims, and the patterns that weren't lining up.

"I've been treating this like a puzzle," she murmured. "But maybe it's not just about the facts. Maybe it's about what's underneath them."

Ben glanced at her. "You've got the instincts to see it. Stop burying them under timelines and reports."

Claire didn't argue.

"Every spoke left behind..." she said slowly, "It's a piece of what holds the whole wheel together. You take it out, and everything wobbles. Every victim, every strike; it's not about warning us. It's about showing what's already broken."

Ben's expression hardened. "So, they're not just killing. They're reenacting something."

"Exactly," she said. "Something that broke them first."

Ben was quiet for a moment. "You're not guessing."

"No," she said softly. "I know the look of someone who's leaving pieces of their pain behind."

They drove in silence; the hum of the engine was low and even. Claire's mind turned to Ryan, his evasiveness, his secrets. "Ryan's tied to all of this," she said. "He's either hiding something or he's terrified he's next."

Ben gave her a sidelong glance. "Which is it?"

"I don't know," Claire admitted. "But I caught him meeting with Dean Harris today. They have been meeting every Thursday."

Ben straightened. "You went?"

"I had to," Claire said. "Dean's still chasing answers about Elliot. He's drowning in grief, but Ryan... Ryan was calm."

"And you trust him?" Ben asked.

"I don't know if I can," Claire said. "But I think he knows more than he's telling."

Ben exhaled loudly. "And Marissa?"

"She's bitter, wounded, but not the killer. Not from what I can see."

Ben's fingers tapped against the dashboard. "And then there's Nessa."

Claire's grip tightened on the wheel. "She's a wildcard. She's not part of the cycling community, but she's everywhere. Always watching. Always talking in riddles. I went to her cabin."

Ben cursed under his breath. "Alone?"

"She wouldn't have opened up if you were there. You know that."

Ben said nothing, but his frown deepened.

"Her drawings," Claire continued. "Cyclists on wooded roads. The lighthouse. She's connected to this. I don't know how, but she is."

Ben shook his head. "She's not just a bystander. She's part of it."

"Next time, we'll both go." Claire said.

"Agreed."

The car fell silent as they passed Haven Café.

"People are scared," Claire remarked. "That's exactly what the killer wants."

"Then we need to find them before the next one falls," Ben said. "Monroe won't give us another week."

The station lights cut through the dark as Claire pulled into the lot. She and Ben got out, the urgency pulsing between them. This wasn't slowing down. It was closing in.

Inside, the building was quiet. Just a few officers in the hallways. Claire led them to the small room they'd claimed as their command center. The table was a mess of photos, scrawled notes, and timelines. The whiteboard showed the town map, its edges curling from heat and time. Red pins marked every crime scene.

Ben moved to the table, his fingers skimming the edge of a photo. "It's how clean they are that gets me," he said. "Not one hair or print. Just the spoke."

"They're erasing everything but the message," Claire replied, staring at the pins. "They want us to see the pattern without ever catching the hand that drew it."

"They know these roads. Every turn, every trailhead. They're watching routines. Waiting for moments no one else would notice."

Claire's focus shifted to the whiteboard. "This isn't just calculated, it's intimate. Someone who understands vulnerability from the inside out. Someone who's been on those roads, who knows what it's like to ride alone and feel seen."

Ben reached for the map from the lighthouse. He looked at it carefully. "This X—blue ink, out by the cliffs. It lines up near the quarry."

Claire stepped closer. "That can't be a coincidence."

Ben looked at her. "You think it's a graveyard?"

"Maybe not literal," Claire said. "But symbolic. That quarry... Everything turns around it."

Ben tapped his knuckle on the table. "That keeps Nessa on the board. She's always nearby. Never the center, but close enough to raise suspicion."

Claire's thoughts drifted back to Nessa's cabin. She could still see the charcoal sketches; the jagged coastline etched with uneasy precision. Not just scenery, something lived in. A memory rendered by hand, too raw to be imagined.

"Nessa draws like someone who can't forget," Claire said quietly. "But that doesn't mean she's the one behind this."

Ben didn't flinch. "And Marissa?"

Claire exhaled. "Isolated. Resentful. But careful. She's too controlled. There's more to her silence."

"She's angry," Ben said. "But is she obsessed?"

Claire didn't answer. She looked at the map again, and the red pins now felt like clock hands ticking. Her jaw clenched.

"There's a sharp mind behind this," she said finally. "A design. We're not just chasing a killer; we're chasing a philosophy."

Ben's brow furrowed. "You're saying it's not just murder. It's doctrine."

Claire's voice dropped. "Every death is a correction. A punishment. Not for crime, but for failure."

They stood in silence, the hum of the fluorescent light a low drone above them.

Then Claire's voice broke through. "You know what I hate most?" she said, fixed on the board.

"It's that I can feel them. I've spent my life trying to stay ahead of chaos, Ben. And this..." her hand gestured to the wall of red pins, the photographs, the shattered spokes "...this feels like it's chasing me back."

Ben didn't speak. He didn't have to. The truth of it hung

between them.

He finally said, "It's Lena, isn't it?"

Claire nodded. "She's next. And I don't think the killer's just planning it. I think they want us to see it coming."

Ben's expression hardened. "We get to her first."

Claire's jaw tightened. "We don't get another chance."

Ben glanced toward the hallway. "Monroe's ready to call it. One more body and it's out of our hands."

Claire turned back to the board. "Then we don't give him one."

Claire's spine straightened. Her fear hadn't diminished, but something sharper was rising to meet it.

The shadows on the road weren't finished yet.

14

Predator's Descent

A figure crouched low in the undergrowth, hidden behind a wall of dew-covered ferns. Every muscle was tense, every sense sharpened. Breathing slowed to a controlled pace.

Lena Crawford was on her usual path. Neon cut through the gray as she followed the familiar curves. Her legs burned with the climb, but she embraced it. The pain meant progress. Meant she was still in the fight. Still chasing the version of herself who didn't flinch. But frustration trailed close behind. Not fast enough. Not good enough. Not yet.

One more hill, she told herself, the thought as ingrained as the ride itself. Push harder. Don't hold back. The night air left her instincts unsettled. She glanced toward the pines, their silhouettes crowding the road. A shiver rippled through her spine.

Get it together, Lena. It's just nerves.

Still, the feeling clung to her. Someone was watching. She tightened her grip on the handlebars, anchoring herself in the motion of her legs and the whisper of tires on asphalt.

From the unseen corners, eyes tracked her movement with predatory patience. A broken spoke rested in a gloved hand. One clean strike. That was all it would take. Not yet, the figure thought. Wait.

Lena crested the hill, her lungs burning. The road stretched ahead, daring her to keep going. She welcomed the challenge. This wasn't just training; it was a test of resolve. A way to silence the voice that told her she'd never be enough.

She passed a sharp bend, the unease gnawing at her again. The trees seemed too still. The predator tensed, but hesitation crept in. She's too fast tonight. Too sharp. The thought stung, an unwelcome reminder of a miscalculation. The opportunity was slipping.

Lena's thoughts drifted briefly to the Classic. The memory of her last race cut deep; the lead she'd lost, the sting of being overtaken in the final stretch. Her jaw clenched, not again. This time, I own the finish line. The drive surged through her, pushing her legs faster.

From the undergrowth, the figure's grip on the spoke tightened, then loosened. There will be another night. A better one.

Lena didn't feel the threat fade. She kept moving. The ride ran longer than planned, but she didn't care. Her body ached, her muscles screamed, but the strain made her feel unbreakable. When she turned the last corner, the sight of Haven Café brought great relief. She slowed, coasting toward the side door.

Lena dismounted, legs shaky from the ride, and leaned her bike against the wall. Without hesitation, she pushed open the side door of the café and stepped into its warmth. The familiar scent of coffee and fresh bread wrapped around her. She exhaled slowly, but the silence wasn't kind; it stirred memories.

She couldn't shake the thought: Am I next? Anger tightened inside her. She hated feeling powerless. If they're watching, let them watch, she thought. I'm still here. I'm not done riding.

Her phone screen glowed briefly as she checked the time. She should have gone home, but the empty house felt lonelier than this café. At least here, there was warmth. A place to breathe.

The faint light of dawn began to color the sky outside. Marie stepped in, her face tired but kind.

"Lena?" she asked, both surprised and concerned. "You okay, hon?"

Lena forced a small smile. "Yeah. Just needed a place to sit for a while."

Marie nodded. "You're always welcome here. Coffee?"

"Please," Lena said.

As Marie prepared for opening, Lena stared through the window, watching the empty street. The heaviness from the ride was easing when the door jingle snapped her back.

Liam stepped in.

"Lena," he said, surprised. "You're here early."

"Morning," she replied, her tone neutral.

Liam stepped inside, pausing when he saw her. He hesitated, then made his way over. "Mind if I sit?" he asked.

When she gave a small nod, he lowered himself into the seat and set his notebook down. "I wasn't expecting to see anyone this morning," he said, voice calm.

"But while I've got the chance... I've been trying to make sense of everything happening out there. People are scared. I want to understand it, not just report on it."

"You think I have answers?" she asked, fingers curling around her cup.

"I think you have perspective," he said gently. "You knew them all. You know what this community feels like from the inside."

She let out a slow breath. "People are dead. That's all that matters."

"And if talking can stop the next death?"

"Talking doesn't change what's coming," she said sharply. "Do you think an article will fix this?"

"I think silence feeds it," he countered.

Lena stared at the dark street outside. "You ever feel like fear isn't new, but something that's just always been there? Waiting?"

Liam hesitated. "You mean now? With everything that's happening?"

"I mean always," she said, then shook her head. "Forget it."

"What about the broken spoke?" he asked softly.

She stiffened. "That's not just a part of a bike. It holds tension and balance. Break it, and the whole thing collapses. Whoever's leaving it... they know where the weak spots are."

"You think it's someone from the inside?" he asked.

"Or someone who remembers how it feels to be out there," she murmured.

He studied her face. "Do you think you're a target?"

She hesitated, then nodded slightly. "We all are. No one wants to admit it, but it's true."

Liam's voice softened. "I'm not here to write gossip. I'm looking for truth."

She stood abruptly, pushing back her chair. "Then you're looking in the wrong place. Truth isn't in interviews."

He called after her, "Then where is it?"

She stopped in the doorway, her back to him. "It's in the moments no one wants to look at. That's where it starts."

Outside, the haze was denser than before. She leaned against the café wall, heart pounding, hands finally still after their tremors earlier.

She hated that everyone saw her as unshakable. She hated how easily she let them believe it.

It wasn't the idea of being next that scared her. It was the feeling that something deeper was unraveling, and no amount of grit or speed could fix it.

She inhaled sharply, pushed off the wall, and rode away. Not fearless but no longer pretending otherwise.

As Liam stepped out of the café, the cold air cut through him. He pulled his coat tighter and slipped the notebook into his pocket. There was a story here, but it wasn't one he could write from a distance.

The walk to the Gazette's office was brisk. Darkness pooled along the sidewalks as if someone were watching. He shook it off and kept moving.

Inside, the office was nearly empty. Fiona was at her desk, her face lit by the glow of her computer screen. Liam headed straight for his. Papers and clippings were scattered every-where.

He pulled a weathered article from the stack; it was fifteen years old. The headline read: *Cyclist Found Dead on Coastal Road.* The details were vague, the tone dismissive. A tragic accident on slick roads, they said. But even then, whispers hinted at something darker.

With a pen in hand, he underlined words that stood out. *Slick roads. Lone cyclist. No witnesses.*

The pattern stirred something in him. Another clipping surfaced; ten years ago, almost to the day, another cyclist died, this time on Route 7. Same language and same undertone of unease.

Liam flipped to a blank page in his notebook, his pen moving fast:

- **15 years ago:** *Fatal cyclist accident. Rumors of foul play.*
- **10 years ago:** *Another cyclist, same conditions, same stretch*

of road.

- **5 years ago:** *Nessa Greene. A witness. Her statement: shadows, something moving. The case went cold.*

He stared at the list, pulse quickening. Every five years, another death. Until now. Now the pattern wasn't a single tragedy; it was a string of murders.

Fiona's voice cut through. "You're muttering again, Harper. Starting to sound like you're onto something."

He looked up. "Every five years, Fiona. Look at this." He slid the papers toward her.

"Fifteen, ten, five… and now this year. These aren't accidents. And the broken spokes? They're deliberate. Like someone saying, *I've been here all along.*"

She leaned over the papers. "You think it's connected?"

"I think it's ritual," Liam said. "Calculated. And five years ago, Nessa Greene was the only one who saw anything. Her statement was a single line, and everyone dismissed her."

"Do you think she knows more?" Fiona asked.

"Maybe she saw too much," Liam replied. "Or maybe she's been living with it ever since."

He jotted another line in his notebook: *Is Nessa a witness or a warning?*

Liam didn't wait any longer. He grabbed his phone, his pulse quickening as he scrolled to Claire's number.

She picked up on the second ring. "Liam?" Claire's tone was guarded.

"I've been digging," he said. "There's a pattern. Fifteen years of deaths, every five years. These new murders... they're not random. It's all connected, Claire."

A pause followed. "You're sure about this?"

"Sure enough to know we've been missing the bigger picture," he said. "I need to show you what I've found."

"Where are you?" she asked.

"At the Gazette. I can come to you."

"Meet me at the station," Claire said. "Bring everything."

"I'm on my way."

He ended the call and grabbed the articles, his notes, his coat, and his keys in one motion. The chill hit him again as he stepped outside, but this time it didn't slow him down. If his hunch was right, the killer's message had been rippling for years, and they were only just starting to hear it.

Liam pulled up to the Police Department, his gaze briefly landing on the stack of articles and notes on the passenger seat. Each yellowed clipping and scrawled line felt alive, part of a story that was finally taking shape.

Inside, the station was calm, the hum of fluorescent lights casting a stark glow across the empty lobby. Claire was waiting near her office, her brow tense with thought. She looked up as he approached and gave a small nod, motioning for him to follow her into the conference room.

"Thanks for meeting me," Liam said as he dropped into the chair across from her. He set down his notebook and a thick folder with a thud. "This isn't something I could explain over the phone."

Claire scanned the disorganized pile. "You said it couldn't wait."

"It can't," Liam replied, his voice firm. He opened the folder and spread out the articles and photographs.

"I've been digging through every file I could find, recent murders, cold cases, and accidents. There's a pattern."

Her expression sharpened. "Show me."

He slid the first clipping across the table. *Cyclist Found Dead on Coastal Road.* The date was fifteen years ago. Claire skimmed it, her jaw tightening.

"Ruled an accident," Liam said, tapping the page. "No witnesses, no evidence. But the details don't match a crash severe enough to kill him. It looks staged."

He pulled out the next clipping. "Ten years ago. Michael Travers. Same time of year, same story. Another accident that doesn't hold up."

Claire looked up, her voice low but pointed. "No one connected these before?"

"The town didn't want panic," Liam said. "They chalked it up to risk. Cyclists crash. It's part of the sport."

"But five years ago..." He hesitated, sliding forward the third article. "Danica Shaw. Nessa Greene was the only witness."

Claire straightened. "She told investigators she saw something. A figure in the fog."

Liam nodded. "One vague statement. Then the case was dropped." He leaned back. "Every five years, Claire. Fifteen. Ten. Five. And now? It's not a single incident anymore. It's a chain of murders."

"Someone is escalating. The broken spokes," she murmured. "It's deliberate. A message."

"Or a warning," Liam countered.

Silence passed between them, heavy with implications.

Claire leaned forward. "Whoever's behind this isn't just killing. They're dismantling the community. It feels like revenge."

Liam's notebook was open again, his pen hovering. "Nessa. Marissa. One of them has to hold the key."

"We're missing something," Claire said, staring at the photo of Danica Shaw's wrecked bike. "A link that explains the pattern."

Liam closed the folder with deliberate care. "We're already running out of time."

Neither moved. This was too heavy. Finally, Liam gathered his notes and stood, the strap of his satchel slung over his shoulder.

"Let me know when you find something," he said. His voice carried both resolve and an undercurrent of frustration.

Claire nodded but didn't speak. She watched him leave. Only when the door closed did she let out a slow breath she hadn't realized she'd been holding.

The table was a mess of papers, timelines, and clippings, but Claire kept looking at one photo: Danica's bike, and that empty stretch of road swallowed by stillness. A minute passed. Maybe two.

The scrape of footsteps on the station's worn floor pulled her from her thoughts. Ben stepped inside, his eyes landing on her instantly. He took in the clutter of files and the sharp focus etched on her face.

"You're deep in it."

Claire straightened, still half in the timeline Liam had laid out. "Yeah," she said softly. "And we're closer than I thought."

Ben pulled out the chair across from her and sat down. "Closer to what?"

She sifted through her notes, "A detail that's been hiding in plain sight."

"Liam gave you something big, didn't he?" Ben asked, leaning against the desk with folded arms.

Claire nodded. "A pattern. Every five years, a cyclist dies under strange circumstances. Fifteen years ago, ten, five... and now we're here again. It sounds far-fetched, but the more I think about it, the more it lines up."

Ben's expression hardened. "Every five years? Whoever's behind this isn't just patient, they're deliberate."

"Exactly. If these deaths started that long ago, there'll be old case files. Probably marked as accidents. We need to find them."

Ben gave a low whistle. "Accidents are easy to dismiss. No one questions them. But every five years? That's a timeline you don't ignore."

He pushed back his chair. "Let's check the archives. Maybe something in those old reports will jump out."

The records room was dim, lined with steel shelves stacked high with forgotten files. Claire pulled down the boxes she needed while Ben opened one marked fifteen years ago. He spread its contents on the table.

"Darren Fletcher," he murmured. "Cyclist. Found dead on the coastal road. Autopsy says poor road conditions caused it. But look at this." He held up a faded photo. "See anything?"

Claire leaned closer. The broken spoke lay near Darren's bike, half-buried in dirt. "There it is," she whispered. "It's not subtle. It was left there, like a marker."

Ben nodded grimly. "Liam's right. This goes way back. Let's look at the one from ten years ago." He flipped open the next file. "Michael Travers. Another cyclist. Found near the cliffs.

Witnesses said he misjudged a turn and went off the road. But...
" He passed Claire a photo. A single broken spoke lay beside the wreckage.

"Whoever did this wanted it to be seen but not understood."

Ben reached for the last file. His jaw tightened as he read. "Danica Shaw. Five years ago. Witnessed by Nessa Greene."

His voice darkened. "And she claimed she saw a figure, but no one believed her."

Claire's lips pressed into a thin line. "Nessa's name keeps surfacing."

"And Marissa?" Ben asked.

"She doesn't fit the five-year cycle. Her accident's too recent. I think she's caught in the middle of this, not behind it."

"Which leaves us with Nessa," Ben said firmly. "She knows these roads. If she's not the one, she knows who is."

Claire turned to another photo; Danica's bike, bent and broken near the cliff's edge. "Whoever this is, they're marking time. Every spoke, every death, they're carving their story into the road."

Ben sat back. "We need to figure out why. Why cyclists? Why this town?"

They sat in silence for a long moment, the photos lined up like evidence of a curse. Claire's voice finally cut through. "Tomorrow is the Classic. Everyone will be there. If the killer wants to send a final message, that's the stage to do it."

Ben's jaw set. "Then we'll be ready. We'll station ourselves along the route, keep watch on the cyclists and the crowds."

"Agreed," Claire said. "We'll stay in constant contact. The

moment anything feels off, we move."

They spent the next hour marking up the route and cross-referencing old maps with the race layout. It was well past midnight when they finally closed the files, exhaustion pulling at their faces.

Claire glanced at Ben. "Tomorrow might be our only chance to stop this."

"Then we won't miss it," Ben said.

They left the station under the cold night sky. Tomorrow wasn't just about the race; it was about finding the person who had been waiting all these years for the perfect moment to strike.

15

Race to the Truth

The early morning air pulsed with anticipation, carrying the scent of damp earth and brewing coffee. Havenport's town square was already awake, alive with the excitement of race day. Cyclists in bright jerseys spun their wheels and adjusted helmets, their voices blending with the chatter of spectators staking out spots along the route.

Claire moved through the crowd, noting the determination on the riders' faces. The atmosphere was festive, but beneath it, she sensed the unrest.

She found Lena across the square, stretching near the starting line, surrounded by a few local racers offering quick words of encouragement. Her face was composed, but Claire caught the subtle tightening of her face. She admired Lena's grit, how she balanced being both a competitor and a potential target.

Ryan was nearby, leaning on his handlebars. The sight of him sent an urgency through Claire. If the killer were going to make a move, this race would be perfect.

As Claire rounded the corner by the old general store, she spotted a lone figure standing apart from the crowd.

Nessa leaned against the building's weathered boards; her dark coat draped around her. A cigarette smoldered between her fingers, its smoke curling lazily upward into the morning light. Her gaze fixed on the cyclists gathering near the start line, the expression on her face caught between disdain and something almost mournful. She tapped the cigarette against her palm in a small, restless rhythm, too sharp to be boredom, too controlled to be fear.

Claire slowed as she approached, weaving through families. "Nessa," Claire greeted, her tone steady, edged with caution.

Nessa tilted her head slightly in acknowledgment, then took a long drag, holding the smoke in her lungs before letting it trail out between her teeth.

"Race day," she said, her voice carrying a brittle undercurrent. "The one day they all crawl out of the woodwork."

She gestured with a flick of her hand toward the racers clustered near the starting line. Her gaze paused on Lena, lingering too long. Something cold cut across her face before she smothered it beneath a scoff.

"Not a fan of the event, I take it?" Claire asked, looking at her carefully.

"Not of the event," Nessa muttered. "And not of the people who think they're better than the rest of us. They speed through like the world bends for them. Like nothing could touch them."

Claire studied her. "You sound like someone who's been touched by it."

Nessa's eyes were flat and unreadable. "I learned early. The roads don't care who you are. They choose who survives."

The words landed between them, quiet but sharp.

Claire felt her pulse tighten, though her expression didn't shift. "That's a bleak way to see it."

"It's the truth," Nessa said simply, like stating the weather. "Some of us stopped pretending otherwise."

Her tone didn't rise. That made it worse.

"Interesting timing," Claire said after a pause, keeping her voice even. "With everything going on, this seems like a day you'd want to stay close. Not slip away."

Nessa's lips curved faintly. "I prefer to keep my distance from anything involving them." Her voice carried a strange finality.

For a fleeting second, Lena's laugh carried across the square, clear and bright. Claire caught it, the change in Nessa's expression. Not envy or grief. Recognition. It was gone before

Claire could pin it down.

Before she could press further, Nessa dropped the cigarette and crushed it under her heel. "Enjoy the show, Claire."

With that, she turned and strode down the back street. Claire stood still, unsettled by the sharp edge in Nessa's voice and the way she had stared at Lena, as though seeing something inevitable. Observing but never participating, that had always been Nessa's way.

Near the starting line, Lena and Ryan were preparing. The sight tugged at something in her chest. There wasn't time to dwell on Nessa now. She checked her watch and headed for the station, her thoughts already shifting to Ben and the plan for the day.

By the time she arrived, he was already at his desk, leaning over a clipboard filled with race participant names, his pen tapping absently against the page. He looked up as she entered.

"Spot anything unusual?"

"I ran into Nessa." She crossed her arms and leaned against his desk. "She claims she's staying away from the race. Said she can't stand being around the cyclists. But the way she said it..."

She shook her head. "There's something darker there, Ben. It's not just an annoyance. It's like she despises them."

Ben let out a low hum. "She does seem to be at the center of everything, doesn't she? Always watching, never being involved. If she's heading home, maybe we should have someone watch her."

"Agreed," Claire said, straightening. "Let's make sure she stays on our radar. This is cutting it too close, especially with both Lena and Ryan in the spotlight today."

He looked up. "We'll get through this," he said firmly.

Across town, the Haven Café was alive. The rich scent of coffee and fresh pastries spilled into the street. By early morning, every seat was filled. The line at the counter stretched to the door as patrons came and went, all drawn by the pull of race day.

Inside, the café was decked out for the occasion. Streamers hung from the windows, and small pennants with numbers of past winners lined the counter. Faded photographs of previous races covered one wall, snapshots of familiar faces crossing the finish line. Near the register, Marie had set out a polished silver trophy; a relic from the year her husband Tom had competed.

Marie moved behind the counter with the efficiency of someone who had seen mornings like this for years. There was a brightness in her that came from more than just routine. She poured coffee, steamed milk, and set out plates of her famous blueberry muffins, all while chatting with customers in her warm, familiar way.

"Marie. Is the competition as fierce as it sounds?" asked Pete, an older man at the counter who leaned on his elbows, looking at the trophy.

Marie smiled, brushing a stray strand of gray hair behind her ear. "Oh, Pete, you know this town. Everyone's got a favorite racer, and they'll argue about it all day if you let them. But I'll tell you this, Lena Crawford's the one to watch. She's been training harder than anyone I've seen in years."

Nearby, a group of teenagers in cycling jerseys crowded around a table, voices lowered as they swapped predictions. "Ryan's gonna take her in the hills," one said with a grin, holding up his phone to show a photo of Ryan from a past race.

The others nodded, a mix of admiration and excitement flashing on their faces.

By the window, Ruth sat in her usual chair, knitting needles clicking steadily as she worked on a scarf in vibrant red.

"Lena's got fire in her," she announced to anyone who would listen. "But that Moore boy, don't count him out. He's got a solemn kind of strength. You can see it in the way he rides. It's not showy."

A couple at the next table leaned closer, speaking just low enough to slip under the hum. "Fire or not, she's pushing her luck," the woman murmured. "The others thought they were untouchable too."

Her companion nodded grimly. "Feels like she's daring it. Like daring the curse to come for her next."

At the counter, someone muttered that the town should've canceled the race this year. That parading around like nothing had happened was asking for trouble. The café's laughter dimmed, like everyone felt it, but no one wanted to be the one to say it out loud.

At a corner table, Liam sat with his notepad open, his pen moving quickly as he jotted down pieces of conversation. He cared less about predictions and more about the current running beneath them. It wasn't just excitement; it was something sharper.

He watched a young boy tug on his father's sleeve, whispering that he wanted to be like Lena someday. Liam scribbled it down with a faint smile, but the smile faded as he caught the father's reply, low and tense:

"Not if you're smart."

Liam paused, his pen hovering.

Admiration, fear, superstition; all braided together so tightly now the town couldn't tell them apart.

The square outside was filling fast, and the crowd's energy felt less like celebration and more like a collective breath being held.

In the back of the café, two men argued over their coffees. "Ryan's got the stamina for the hills," one said, tapping the table with conviction. "But if Lena keeps her pace even, she'll take him in the sprint."

"It's all timing," the other countered. "One mistake and it's all over."

As the clock crept toward the start of the race, the café began to empty. Patrons finished their drinks and pulled on jackets, eager to secure the best viewing spots along the route. Marie called out the last few orders while even the regulars drifted toward the door.

Liam studied his notes, then snapped the notebook shut. The facts meant nothing without context, just noise. He pocketed the pen and stood, heading to the counter where Marie moved with her usual, practiced precision.

He hesitated. "Thanks, Marie."

She looked up, her expression tired but knowing. "Enjoy the race, Liam."

He nodded, then turned and stepped outside.

The main street was a slow-moving current of people funneling toward the barricades. Music from the loudspeakers blew through the air.

Off to the side, on a bench half in shadow, sat an older man in a faded team jacket. His hands were knotted over the head of a cane, his posture still carrying a trace of the athlete he'd once been. Liam recognized him, Harold Pierce, a name buried deep in the archives. A local champion, back when the race had drawn crowds from across the county.

Liam approached. "Didn't think you came out for these anymore."

Harold's mouth twitched. "Didn't think anyone remembered I used to."

"I do," Liam said, sitting on the edge of the bench. "I'm writing about the race. About what it means to this town."

Harold's gaze stayed on the road where the first riders were warming up. "It used to mean everything. Pride. Belonging. You won, and you were part of this place forever."

"And now?"

"Now they win, and they think it makes them untouchable." His voice was quiet, but hard around the edges. "But the roads don't care. They always take back their kings."

Liam stilled, pen forgotten in his hand.

Harold finally looked at him. His eyes were pale and sharp. "Ask anyone who's been here long enough. The higher they rise, the harder the roads come for them. They don't forget. They just wait."

The words hung between them.

Liam stood slowly. "Thanks for the perspective."

Harold gave a small nod, already turning his gaze back to the asphalt, like he was watching ghosts line up for the start.

Liam moved back into the flow of the crowd. Turning onto the main street, he almost ran into Ben. The easygoing nature Ben often carried was gone; he looked like a man on a mission.

"Sergeant," Liam said, stepping aside.

Ben gave him a curt nod. "Looking for a headline?"

"Not a headline," Liam replied, his tone clipped. "A pattern. This race feels... wrong. Like it's more than just a race."

Ben's voice was low. "People are on edge. That café back there? Half the town's whispering about the Ghost Rider. Fear's already running high, Harper. Don't add fuel."

Liam didn't back down. "You know as well as I do that something's off. Every five years? It's not a coincidence, Ben. Nessa was there for at least one of them."

He paused, watching for any reaction. "You think she's just an eccentric bystander? Because I don't."

Ben's jaw tightened. He didn't answer right away. "Nessa's on my radar," he said finally. "That's all I'll tell you. Don't get yourself in trouble by poking too hard."

"I saw her earlier," Liam pressed. "She said she was heading home to avoid the 'nasty cyclists,' but I don't believe her. If you're watching her, you'd better keep your eyes wide open."

Ben gave him a long look. "We'll handle it," he said, his tone final. "Stay out of the way, Harper."

Liam's expression hardened, but he didn't push. "Just... be careful, Ben. Whoever's behind this isn't improvising."

Ben gave a short nod and moved on. Liam stood for a moment, watching his retreating figure. His body language said it all; he wasn't dismissing Liam's instincts, not entirely.

As Ben walked to his car, the sounds of race day buzzed around him. It felt wrong, too cheerful given what they had discovered. Nessa's name circled in his mind as he slid into the driver's seat. He looked at the crowd ahead, unaware of what might be coming.

He drove slowly, mapping the quickest route to Nessa's cottage. If she had lied, he needed to know why. Ben parked his car near an overgrown maple and walked towards the cottage. The chipped paint and leaning porch made it feel left behind.

Crouching behind a spruce, Ben waited. There was movement inside, and Nessa appeared in the doorway, her hand remaining on the knob. For a moment, she hesitated. Then she put on her coat and stepped outside, locking the door behind her with deliberate precision.

Ben's pulse rose. So much for staying home.

He followed from a safe distance as she wove through narrow back streets, skirting the gathering crowds along the main road. Her pace was brisk but contained, head low beneath the brim of her hat.

At the edge of the course, she veered into a grove of trees and climbed a low rise that overlooked the starting line. Ben ducked behind a nearby trunk, close enough to study her face without drawing attention.

Nessa stood motionless, arms crossed tight against her chest, locked on the racers below. She didn't scan the crowd. She didn't cheer. Her attention moved only between Lena Crawford and Ryan Moore, back and forth, like she was tracking something only she could see.

The announcer's voice carried across the course, calling the racers forward. Cheers erupted, a wave of sound washing over the crowd, but Ben barely heard it. His gaze was fixed on Nessa. She didn't flinch or smile; her expression was unreadable. But something in her posture had shifted.

This wasn't just a race anymore. It was the start of something else. Something that had already begun.

16

Edge of the Unknown

The buzz of anticipation grew as the crowd pressed in along the race route, spilling onto the street. Cyclists made last-minute gear checks, moving with practiced urgency. Club jerseys added color to the gray morning, flashes of red and neon slicing through the mist.

At the front, Lena and Ryan waited in silence. Lena scanned the opening stretch, already racing it in her mind. Ryan moved with ease, exchanging nods and encouraging words, but Claire caught the way he kept glancing at Lena; respectful, competitive, maybe even protective.

From the trees above, Nessa watched like a hawk. A cigarette burned low between her fingers, smoke curling around her face. She didn't move. She continued to track Lena and Ryan with unsettling precision.

Beside her, Ben tensed. Something about the stillness in Nessa's body made his skin prickle.

The announcer's voice cut through the speakers. "Racers! On your mark!"

The crowd hushed. Cyclists leaned forward, muscles coiled. The whistle blew.

The pack surged ahead; gears clicked, tires hummed, and cheers erupted as the front riders shot forward, Lena and Ryan leading the charge.

Ben felt a flicker of excitement, but it vanished when he found Nessa again. She hadn't moved. She was still watching, like she was waiting for something.

The race wound through Havenport's narrow streets, the energy of the crowd rippling. Flags waved, hands clapped, and the scent of autumn leaves mixed with the warmth of coffee drifted from Haven Café.

Claire stood at the curb, scanning both the race and the crowd. Her phone buzzed with a text from Ben: *She's out by the trees. Watching everything.* Claire looked toward the tree line. Nessa was there, half-hidden, her face unreadable.

Around Claire, familiar faces filled the scene. Marie handed out steaming cups of cider, cheeks pink from the chill. Jasper was manning a small booth, calling out for folks to grab a snack.

Liam scribbled notes on a fresh page, his handwriting jagged from trying to watch and write at once. Marissa stood nearby, arms crossed, her expression caught between longing and detachment.

"Thinking about getting back into it?" Liam asked, voice pitched low.

Marissa shook her head, still watching the racers. "Not like this. I know that feeling, pushing yourself, chasing the rush. It's different now."

Liam jotted the words down, though her tone snagged him. There was bitterness beneath the calm.

Further down, Millie waved her handkerchief like a banner, shouting encouragement. Tommy, the eternal commentator, hollered advice at the riders he recognized.

"Hold your line! Don't burn it all on the first lap!" he barked, though most were too deep in the effort to hear.

The lead pack flew past in a tight blur of color, cranks spinning like machinery. Ryan tucked low, Lena glued to his wheel, their cadence matched like mirror images.

The circuit looped out of town along the cliffs and back through the square, about two and a half miles each lap. Seven laps total. The crowd roared as they passed, but under the cheer, there was something sharper.

Liam caught the way people leaned forward too far, flinching as the riders swept by. Like they weren't watching a race; they were bracing for impact.

He glanced at Marissa. Her jaw was locked. Claire's head swept constantly from racers to crowd to the tree line.

Her phone buzzed. *Nessa hasn't moved. She's watching like she's waiting for someone.*

Claire looked toward the trees. Nessa stood rooted at the course edge, smoke curling from the cigarette in her hand, perfectly still. Not watching the race, watching its shape. Waiting.
  Claire's gut tightened.

Ryan pushed the hills; Lena clawed back on the descents. The pack stretched thin. Liam's pen hovered uselessly as he tracked their duel. It wasn't just competition. It looked like a collision waiting to happen.

He leaned toward Marissa. "If this pace holds, someone's going to break."

Marissa didn't look at him. "Maybe that's the point."

Liam wrote it down, the words cutting sharper than he expected.

The square trembled with noise. The air tasted like hot asphalt and nerves. Liam could feel the shift, the cheering too tight, the smiles brittle.

He caught whispers in the crowd. *She's pushing too hard. This is how they fall.* He wrote the line fast before it slipped away.

Ryan and Lena were still locked together, like the road itself had narrowed to just the two of them. Tommy's voice cracked as he shouted, "Save something for the finish! Don't cook your legs now!"

A near miss on the corner, Ryan's rear tire twitched and caught, and the crowd's gasp rolled like a wave. Liam's heart slammed. Every instinct screamed trap. The cadence was too perfect, the symmetry unnatural. Like something hidden in the rhythm, waiting.

Claire didn't blink. Her gaze kept darting back to the trees.

Ryan surged. Lena clawed back again. Their wheels nearly kissed. The others had fallen far behind. This was theirs now.

The crowd noise thinned into a tense, ragged hum. It felt less like cheering and more like a collective breath. Ryan and Lena tore past, shoulder to shoulder, faces carved with exhaustion, legs piston-tight with fury.

Claire's heart hammered. Lena's jaw was set, her whole frame taut. Ryan edged closer, handlebars nearly brushing as they hit the final curve.

The crowd erupted, one wall of sound as Lena flung everything she had into the pedals and edged past Ryan by inches, crossing the finish line first.

A shockwave of cheers ripped across the square.

Ryan coasted beside her, both gasping, sweat dripping from their helmets. He held out a hand. She reached for it with a grin, then froze. Her eyes shot toward the tree line. Toward Nessa.

And in that instant, her foot missed the ground. The other caught the top tube. She twisted awkwardly and went down hard, the crack of her helmet against pavement slicing through the noise.

Gasps tore from the crowd.

Ryan dropped to one knee. "Lena!"

She pushed him away, sitting up slowly. "I'm fine," she mumbled, though her voice trembled.

Claire was already moving, pushing through the spectators. She saw Lena's hands shake as she adjusted her helmet, but more than that, she saw her staring at the place where Nessa had stood.

Only now, the space beneath the trees was empty.

Claire's phone buzzed. *She's walking. Just left. No rush. Like nothing happened.*

Claire stared at the trees, her breath catching. Something had shifted. Not just in Lena. Not just in the race, but in the way Nessa timed her movements. The control she held. And the sudden chill in the air.

And it wasn't over, not even close.

The celebration moved to Millie's Diner, where the warmth of fresh coffee and fried bacon hung in the air. The clatter of plates and hum of conversation rose in waves, almost frantic in their cheer.

Lena sat at the center of it all, cheeks flushed, hair still damp with sweat. Her winner's glow sat uneasily on her shoulders, like she wasn't sure how to wear it.

Ryan leaned back beside her, arms folded, the edge of competition still flickering in his eyes. Around them, the locals gathered like a proud family, voices bright and too loud, each laugh cutting sharper than it needed to.

Jasper raised his coffee in a toast, his grin wide. "Lena, that last stretch was unreal! Thought Ryan had you for sure."

Ryan laughed, shaking his head. "She got me fair and square. I guess I need to double my training if I'm ever going to keep up with her."

Lena smirked faintly. "Don't blame me if you can't handle the hills, Ryan."

The table erupted with laughter, louder than the joke deserved.

Millie swept in, topping off mugs with her usual flourish, but her smile faltered at the edges.

"You two gave this town something to cheer about. We needed that," she said warmly. "Too many dark clouds hanging over us lately. You cut right through them."

For a moment, the laughter thinned. People glanced at each other, quick and small, like they were afraid of breaking the spell. Then someone turned up the jukebox. Music burst from the corner, and the noise surged back, forced and bright.

Lena's hand tightened around her mug.

Ryan noticed, leaning slightly toward her. "Are you okay?" he murmured.

Lena gave a quick nod, forcing a smile. "Yeah. Just tired. It's nothing."

Across the diner, Liam sat alone at the counter, turning his coffee slowly in his hands. He watched the scene like it was a photograph; everyone smiling too hard, laughing too fast, daring tragedy not to come back through the door.

They weren't celebrating survival. They were trying to convince themselves it had actually happened.

From outside, Claire caught the exchange. She recognized the look in Lena's eyes, the practiced mask of someone pretending to be fine while something deeper churned beneath. She and Ben leaned against her car, the diner's warm light spilling over them.

Lena's laughter carried through the glass, and Ryan sat close by, smiling at something Jasper said. The warmth of the room contrasted sharply with the unease that never left Claire's chest.

"We can't ignore it," Claire murmured, scanning the glass. "Nessa's always there, circling like a vulture. And this five-year pattern, Liam's not wrong. She's wrapped up in it, one way or another."

Ben's jaw tightened. "We'll keep her close. But I'm not sure she's the only one we need to watch. Someone's setting the pieces, Claire. She might just be one of them."

Claire looked over at Ryan. He was laughing with Lena. He wasn't just another rider chasing the thrill of the race; there was something deeper there, an awareness of the danger.

"He gets it," Claire said, almost to herself.

Ben raised an eyebrow. "Ryan?"

"He feels it too," she replied. "Maybe not all of it, but I can see it in the way he watches the crowd... like he's waiting for something to happen."

Ben crossed his arms, considering her words. "Maybe that's why he's still standing. People like him listen to their gut. I can respect that."

He glanced back at her. "You trust him?"

Claire hesitated. "I don't know if trust is the word," she said finally, her voice softer. "But I think he understands what we're up against. That's something."

When Ben left to follow up on leads, Ryan stepped outside, the laughter and conversation trailing after him. He wore a faint smile, the kind that looked earned rather than easy.

"Guess we survived the day," he said, his tone light but carrying a thread of sincerity.

Claire crossed her arms and leaned back against her car, watching him with a mix of amusement and wariness. "Barely. You and Lena looked ready to tear each other apart out there."

Ryan chuckled, his hand raking through his hair. "It's always been that way with us. She's fire on the bike. Pushes me harder than anyone else ever could."

His voice softened. "But today... I don't know. Something about it felt different. Like the road itself was watching."

Claire tilted her head slightly, studying him. "The road?"

"Maybe I'm imagining things," Ryan said, shrugging. "But it's not just about the race anymore. You can feel it, can't you? That... tension in the air."

The way he said it caught her off guard. It wasn't the voice of someone oblivious; it was someone who'd noticed the same unease she carried.

"Every day," Claire admitted. "That's why I don't get to switch it off. People expect me to hold it all together. So, I do. Because someone has to."

Ryan took a step closer. "Doesn't it get heavy? Carrying all of that on your own?"

Claire felt the answer in her chest before she spoke it. Of course it does. It weighed on her every morning, every sleepless night. But saying that aloud felt like weakness.

She looked away for a moment. "You learn to carry it. There's no other choice."

His hand brushed her arm, a light, fleeting touch, but it anchored her more than she expected. "You don't always have to do it alone," he said softly.

The words sank between them. Part of her wanted to believe him, to let someone share the burden even for a moment. But she couldn't ignore the darkness that still covered Havenport. Not yet.

Her voice dipped lower. "Ryan... if anything happens, if things start closing in around you..." She stopped herself, the next words sticking.

She swallowed them back. "...I need you to tell me. Before it's too late."

Ryan's eyes searched hers. "That sounds like more than just

concern.”

“Maybe it is,” Claire said. Her tone was even, but something in it trembled.

Ryan hesitated, his jaw tightening. “Maybe I do know something. Or maybe I just know what it’s like to keep too much inside until it breaks you.”

For a moment, neither of them spoke. The air felt charged with something unspoken, an understanding, maybe even the beginning of trust.

“Stay close to Lena,” Claire said finally, her voice softer but firm. “And to me, if anything feels off. You’re too close to this, Ryan. I need you safe.”

Ryan’s lips curved into a faint, bittersweet smile. “You always sound like you’re carrying the whole town on your shoulders.”

“Maybe I am,” she said.

She stepped back, the space between them filling again. “Be careful out there,” she said quietly. “This isn’t over.”

Ryan walked home through the streets, the cheers and chatter of Millie’s Diner fading behind him. Lena’s victory replayed in his mind, but so did the look on Claire’s face when the crowd parted. It wasn’t just a race for her. Marissa’s face would not leave his thoughts either. Seeing her in the crowd had rattled him.

He reached his building, the streetlight shining across the pavement. The town felt empty as he unlocked his apartment and stepped inside. The walls were lined with his past, race photos, finish-line smiles, reminders of when life was simpler, and the roads felt safe.

He was drawn to Marissa's picture. Young and vibrant, everything she wasn't anymore. Ryan felt a strange clarity. The accident hadn't just taken Marissa off the road. It had taken something from all of them. The fractures were deeper than anyone wanted to admit.

Claire's words replayed in his head from earlier. *Be careful out there. This isn't over.*

He moved to the window, looking out onto the street below. A figure seemed to stand just beyond the pool of light. His breath caught. He blinked, and the figure was gone.

Ryan stepped back from the window, heart thudding. It wasn't just paranoia. He could feel it now, the way the air seemed to shift, the way the night held on too long. Someone was out there, waiting. And he was done ignoring it.

V

Final Reckoning

17

Shattered Veil

The morning light penetrated the blinds in the Police Department, casting eerie beams across the room. Detective Sandoval sat at her desk; her concentration fixed on the evidence board. The faces of the victims stared at her. Each one is connected by invisible threads with two names at the center of their investigation. Nessa Greene and Marissa Lane.

Ben entered, coffee in hand, and handed one to Claire. He took his place beside her, and they studied the board together. The photographs, notes, and red strings formed a web of connections that remained incomplete.

Ben took a deep breath and locked onto the first photo. "Victor Romero. The confident leader of the cycling community. He was the one who called Nessa out publicly after she mocked that rally, right? The one held at the end of the season last year."

Claire nodded. "He was more than that. Victor wasn't confident; he was determined. Believed cycling could put Havenport on the map. A way to draw people in and boost local businesses. He wanted cyclists to have priority on the roads."

"And Nessa... she didn't simply dislike that idea. She hated it. She called him arrogant more than once, even told him that cyclists like him didn't belong here."

Ben leaned forward. "Victor didn't back down. He pushed for designated lanes and more visibility for cyclists. I can see why he would be a target for Nessa.

"But what about Marissa? He knew her, too."

"True," Claire agreed, looking at Victor's smiling face in the photograph. "Marissa and Victor had been friends once, when she was racing. He encouraged her, even coached her a bit. After her accident, they drifted apart. Victor moved on to foster new talent, and Marissa saw it as betrayal. He represented a world that moved on without her."

Ben shook his head. "We've got Victor, someone who clashed with both. But Nessa's hostility feels different. It wasn't irritation; it was targeted. She didn't just dislike him; she wanted him silenced."

Claire hesitated, then flipped over a note tucked beneath Victor's clipping. "Lena said something once, before the races picked up again this season. She told me Victor believed in community, if you keep up... Slow down, and you're out."

Ben lifted a brow. "Sounds like admiration, but also resent-ment."

"It was both," Claire said. "People respected him. Some even loved him. But there was always pressure. Victor set the bar high and expected everyone to reach it. If you needed time or support, he didn't always make space for that."

She looked back at the board, at the bold lines connecting names and dates.

"He thought he was lifting people," she added. "And maybe he was. But sometimes even the helping hand can feel like a shove."

They moved to the next photograph: Elliot Harris, a young, reckless cyclist known for his daring stunts and brash confi-dence.

"Elliot was a risk-taker," Claire began, her tone careful. "He ignored the rules and cut corners. Nessa would have seen him as a menace. Someone who thought he owned the roads. And she did more than complain about him."

"I spoke to a witness who remembers Nessa shouting at him a few months ago, saying he'd be the death of someone one day."

"Like she was predicting his end," Ben murmured. "Marissa knew him, too, didn't she?"

Claire sighed, glancing at her notes. "Not closely, but she knew him. Elliot idolized her when he was younger, when she was at the peak of her career. He tried to get her attention after the accident. She pushed him away. Probably saw him as a reminder of everything she'd lost. Youth, freedom, that invincible feeling."

Ben nodded, flipping through one of the interview transcripts. "His friend Carter Winslow said something I keep thinking about. He told us everyone saw Elliot as fearless, but that's not what he was. He wasn't racing because he loved the risk. He was trying to stay ahead of whatever was catching up to him."

Claire looked up slowly. Ben continued.

"Carter said riding with him felt like chasing a fire that didn't care if it burned out. You couldn't help but follow him. But you also knew, sooner or later, he'd go too far."

Claire let the words settle as she drifted back towards the evidence board. Elliot's photo sat tilted under a pin, not quite straight. She didn't fix it.

All this time, she'd devoted her attention to behavior, patterns, and timelines. But this; this was something else. There was grief in Carter's words, the kind that didn't come from losing a daredevil, but from watching someone self-destruct slowly while the world applauded their fearlessness.

She picked up her pen, then set it down again.

"We've been looking at him as reckless," she said. "But maybe what made him vulnerable wasn't the risk. It was the silence behind it. No one asked why he rode like that."

Ben didn't speak. He didn't need to.

Claire turned back to the board, but her thoughts were somewhere else entirely. The story wasn't just in the evidence. It was in the spaces between it. In the people, and the parts no one wanted to say out loud.

And maybe that's where the truth was waiting.

Ben nodded. "Elliot had ties to both but was more direct with Nessa. To Marissa, he might have been a painful reminder. But to Nessa, he was a nuisance, one she might have wanted gone."

They moved on to Megan Sharpe, the heart of the cycling community, a woman loved by nearly everyone.

Claire's tone softened. "Megan was the glue that held everyone together. She was a mentor and a friend. Nessa seemed to hold a special resentment toward her, always calling her 'too soft' and accusing her of being naïve. She called her efforts to build the community a 'fool's errand.' Her kindness seemed to make Nessa's contempt worse."

Ben tapped his pen against the table. "And yet, Megan wasn't a threat to Nessa. Not in the way the others were. So why would Nessa want her gone?"

"Maybe because Megan was everything she couldn't be," Claire said. "Or maybe because she had a strength that Nessa didn't understand. A power that drew people to her."

She paused, looking at the photo pinned to the board. The warmth radiated from it, even now.

"There was a night at the community center," Claire added. "A couple of months before Megan died. Elliot and Victor had gotten into it. Nothing dramatic, just sharp. It was the kind of moment where things start to shift. She stepped in before it could escalate. She pulled them aside after the meeting and reminded them why the group mattered.

I remember her voice. She said, "If we stop believing the best in each other, we've already lost."

Ben looked over. "Sounds like her."

Claire nodded. "She meant it. She always believed people could come back together. That one conversation, one act of grace, could close any divide."

She hesitated.

"But grace isn't always enough. That moment should have been a warning. Something was breaking. Instead of forcing anyone to confront it, Megan tried to smooth it over. Make it manageable. Make it safe."

Ben's voice was hushed. "Safety can feel like truth if you need it badly enough.”

Claire's expression changed slightly. “She gave them that. A version of the truth they could live with. And maybe that's why people clung to her. But by protecting them from the cracks, she let them grow deeper. She didn't see that keeping the peace sometimes meant letting the danger in.”

Ben tilted her head, considering her. “And what about Marissa?”

Claire sighed, a trace of sadness on her face. “They were close once. But after the accident, everything shifted. The bitterness crept slowly. Watching someone else step into a leadership role, organizing rides and keeping the community together, only reminded her of what she'd lost.”

“Megan kept reaching out, offering chances to stay involved. Marissa declined every invitation. To her, those efforts felt like reminders instead of kindness. To Megan, it was never about control. It was simply a refusal to give up on a friend who had already let go.”

Ben frowned with a hint of frustration. “Both of them would've had reason to want her out of the way. One resented her efforts, the other envied her resilience.”

They moved to Derek Marshall, a seasoned cyclist. He had a reputation for being methodical and precise.

“Derek was a disciplined man, cautious. He clashed with Nessa on safety issues and road-sharing rights. He wasn't rude, but he didn't hold back either. They argued more than once, mostly about her lack of respect for cyclists."

Ben nodded. "But Marissa... she trained with him before her accident, right?"

"She did," Claire replied. "Derek and Marissa weren't close. They respected each other. After the accident, though, that shifted. Derek wanted to help; Marissa became distant. She wouldn't take his calls, wouldn't accept his help. To Derek, cycling was about structure and control. Everything that kept him grounded. To Marissa, that structure was a reminder of her broken dreams."

Ben adjusted. "Derek symbolized two different things to them. An obstacle to Nessa, a former ally who became a stranger to Marissa."

They reached the last photograph: Jacob Whitley, young and idealistic. He wanted to expand cycling's presence.

"Jacob had big plans," Claire said. "He wanted to bring in more riders and make a landmark for cyclists. He saw the future, and Nessa saw it as an invasion. She hated him, called him a tourist magnet."

Ben shook his head. "She had open contempt for him... And Marissa?"

Claire sighed. "Jacob was less of a reminder to her, but he

represented a version of the cycling community that she could no longer be part of. Marissa watched him from a distance. She was... dismissive. He was the kind of cyclist she might have liked once, but now he was another person she'd pushed away."

The room fell silent, each connection landing with force as they absorbed the details surrounding each death.

"It's like both of them have reasons for each victim," Claire explained. "Nessa's resentments are more public, more obvious. Marissa's are softer, personal, and more intimate. But Nessa's connection to each death feels deliberate."

"It feels like Nessa's our main suspect. Especially with the 5-year pattern."

Claire nodded, her instincts warning her that a crucial piece was missing. "Agreed. keep a close watch on Lena. See if either of them, or someone connected to them, makes a move."

They shared a long look, their doubts hanging in silence.

Ben spoke first, leaning forward. "We can't wait any longer, Claire. If there's one thing I know, it's that Lena's at risk. She's one of the most well-known riders. She often speaks out about growing the cycling community. If we're going to catch this murderer, we need to be close to her."

Claire nodded. "Agreed. Lena's the natural next target. Especially to someone like Nessa, who saw her as a symbol of everything she despised."

Ben sighed, rubbing his temples. "So, how do we watch Lena without tipping anyone off? We need to be invisible." He took a sip of coffee, deep in thought. "She can't know we're watching her. And neither can anyone else."

Claire tightened her lips, considering. "Ben, if Nessa's watching Lena, and I'm sure she is, it'll be subtle. She'll stay at the edges, out of sight. We'd need to keep an eye on Lena's routines. Nessa has always watched the cycling community from a distance."

Ben paused, rubbing his chin. "And if she's watching us as closely as we're watching Lena, this could get tricky. We'll need decoys, ways to keep watching without tipping our hand."

He tilted his head, studying her. "You're thinking Nessa's not alone, aren't you?"

Claire's fingers tapped absently against her notebook. "I can't shake the feeling that something's off. This whole thing feels layered. Nessa's resentment is obvious, but the precision feels calculated. If she's acting alone, I'd expect more chaos, more emotion. But this? It's like someone's orchestrating it. Someone could be using Nessa's anger as the perfect cover."

Ben let out a long breath. "So, we watch Lena. We watch Nessa; we stay open to the possibility of a third."

They spent the next hour finalizing their plan, carefully sketching the details. Claire and Ben would maintain a physical distance from Lena yet keep constant surveillance. Undercover officers would monitor Lena's usual routes, blending in as regular patrons at Millie's Diner. As joggers along her cycling paths, even as customers browsing the shops.

They would also position plainclothes officers near Nessa's cabin, watching for unusual movement. Nessa's routine was predictable. Early morning walks, afternoons at her secluded cabin on the outskirts, evenings where she sometimes drifted into town, watching from a distance.

Ben reviewed the setup one last time, his expression tightening with determination. "If Nessa tries anything, we'll catch her. Or at least find out who else is in play."

Claire nodded, looking down at her notes. She could feel the presence beyond her reach. A clue that hadn't surfaced in the evidence yet. It was an instinct she couldn't ignore, a warning that the truth they sought was deeper.

"I know we're close, Ben," she said. "But be ready. If we're right about an accomplice, we could be looking at someone closer to the center of this than we think."

Ben nodded. "If there's more to this, Claire, we'll find it. And whoever's hiding won't stay hidden for long."

They gathered their materials as they readied themselves for the days to come. As they prepared to set their trap, Claire couldn't shake the feeling that the darkness was watching, waiting for them to make the first move.

A knock on the door surprised them. Claire and Ben paused over their notes as Liam stepped in, notebook in hand, with that familiar look on his face. The one Claire knew too well. He didn't show up uninvited unless he had a damn good reason.

"Sandoval. Foster," he nodded, his usual dry tone edged with urgency.

Liam sat without wasting time, flipping open his notebook and smoothing the pages like he couldn't get to them fast enough. "I've been digging," he tapped his pen. "Hard. And I've found a few things I think you'll want to hear."

Ben raised a brow. "You always think that Liam."

"Yeah," Liam flashed a faint grin. "But this time, I'm pretty sure I'm right."

Claire crossed her arms, waiting. "Start talking."

He took a breath. "Okay. First, Marissa. We know she's been bitter since the accident, but it goes deeper. Megan Sharpe funded her recovery. Rehab, a personal trainer, the works. Poured money and time into her."

"Megan?" Claire cut in. "She was supporting her?"

"She was," Liam nodded. "But Marissa bailed. Cut ties after

a few months and stopped returning calls. From what people are saying, she felt like Megan was trying to make her into a project instead of a person."

Ben snorted. "Sounds about right. Marissa's never been one to let anyone tell her what to do."

"Yeah," Liam agreed. "And Megan didn't get the memo. She pushed too hard, and Marissa shut her out. Some say she took it as a betrayal. Like she was using her for a comeback story."

Claire let that settle for a second.

Liam nodded, flipping the page. "Then there's Nessa."

Ben leaned forward. "What about her?"

"This is where it gets interesting," Liam said. "I found out Nessa wasn't always the recluse we know now. Twenty years ago, she was part of the cycling community. Briefly, but it's there."

Claire's brow furrowed. "Part of it, how? She raced?"

"No," Liam shook his head. "Not racing. But she was involved. She volunteered with the Cycling Club for about a year. Maintenance stuff and helping with events. She even mapped some of the trail routes they still use."

Ben blinked. "That's a hell of a connection."

"Yeah, and then she vanished from it. No more events, no mention of her. Like she cut the cord and never looked back."

Claire's voice sharpened. "Something happened."

"It must have," Liam agreed. "Because after that, she started pulling away from everyone. Fast forward to now, they don't just annoy her, they haunt her."

Ben swore under his breath. "And nobody saw this before?"

"Nobody cared to look," Liam shook his head. "She blends into the background, and people let her stay there."

Ben's jaw tightened. "So, what now?"

"We keep digging," Claire leaned forward. "We figure out what drove Nessa away. And why Marissa turned on Megan."

Liam closed his notebook and stood. "If it's one of them, they're not done." Liam gave a small nod and turned to leave.

18

Ambiguous Resolution

By midday, Claire and Ben had received at least a half-dozen calls, each stranger than the last. The details were always the same: Nessa wandering through town like a ghost. People said she appeared and disappeared without a sound.

An edge clung to her presence, a familiar disturbance that left people uneasy. A wavering pulse ran through the way she moved, restless yet intent, as if she carried a purpose no one could figure out.

One sighting had her standing by the old stone bridge, leaning on the rail, staring into the dark water below. She was there for nearly an hour. Some swore they saw her lips moving, whispering to someone. A passerby who got too close thought she lifted her head, staring at them or straight through them.

Later, she was seen outside the café. Not inside, she was across the street. People thought she was watching and waiting. Her gaze locked on the door, tracking every cyclist who came and went with an unsettling intensity.

By afternoon, someone spotted her by the cliffs along the coastal road. She stood there, motionless. People who saw her said she was in a trance. Her head tilted, listening to a sound no one else could hear.

Nessa was not wandering around town; she was haunting it. She moved from place to place, following a path that seemed chaotic, yet deliberate. Everywhere she went, the feeling followed.

Claire sat at her desk, staring at the reports, Nessa's every move clinging to her like strands of a tightening web. It was as if she were being drawn into a game. The sightings had formed a map in her mind, each breadcrumb leading somewhere she could not yet see.

"She is not out there by chance," Claire murmured. "She is marking places, mapping a path."

Ben, who had been reading over her shoulder, nodded. "It is like she is performing. Like she wants us to see her."

Claire leaned back, her mind racing. "Why now? Why is she being so visible, so deliberate? This feels like she is trying to tell us a message or lead us somewhere."

Ben frowned, concentrating on the latest report. "Maybe she knows we are watching her, and she is taunting us. Or maybe," he hesitated, "maybe she is trying to reveal a truth only she can see."

"She talks about the fog like it holds secrets, like it is alive," Claire's voice dropped slightly. "It's like she believes it's guiding her. She is drawn to these places, convinced they hold pieces of a larger story."

Claire's skin crawled. Nessa's cryptic words, her strange obsession with shadows and silence, and how she slipped away unnoticed made her seem almost otherworldly. All of it added to the sense of unease that had woven itself through the town.

Ben shifted, glancing toward the window. "If that's true, then whatever she's trying to show us, she does not want it hidden anymore. She's revealing herself, Claire, but why?"

They sat quietly, Nessa's presence hanging over them even though she was miles away. Claire could not shake the feeling that they were being drawn into an old darkness, one that had waited patiently to resurface.

As evening edged closer, the station lights felt too bright, the air too still.

The town had gone quiet by the time Lena found herself lingering outside the Haven Café. Marie had long since locked up, the windows dark, but Lena sat on the steps with her helmet still in her hands.

The street was empty. Even the crickets seemed to have gone silent.

Her legs ached in that familiar way that usually felt like proof of progress. Tonight, it only felt like evidence she had pushed too close to something she could not name.

Her bike leaned against the wall beside her. Just seeing it made her chest tighten. She had trained all year for the Classic, every ride an act of devotion. Lately, the roads felt less like freedom and more like an open invitation for something waiting in the dark.

She traced a finger over a chip in the paint on her handlebars. What if this is no longer worth it?

She tried to picture stopping, putting the bike away for good, but her mind would not hold the image. The road was the only place she felt like herself. Right now, even that felt like borrowed time.

After a long moment, she stood and wheeled her bike home, the faint hum of her tires carrying down the block and thinning into the night.

As evening closed in, Claire and Ben knew they could not wait any longer. Without a word, they stood and headed out. It was time to confront Nessa before she disappeared again.

Claire knocked firmly on the door, her pulse quickening. Nessa opened it; her expression was sharp and unreadable, and as she studied them, a faint smile formed at the corners of her mouth.

"Detectives," she greeted them. "I was wondering when you

would come."

Claire exchanged a look with Ben before speaking. "Nessa, we've had several reports of you around town today. People are seeing you along Lena Crawford's routes, near places tied to the recent murders."

Nessa's eyes sparkled with amusement, her lips curving into a knowing smile. "Yes, I imagine they would. The mist carries whispers, doesn't it? And the darkness, it has a way of bringing things to the surface."

Ben's expression tightened. "Nessa, we are not here to talk in riddles. This is serious. You have been seen watching Lena, and we want to know why."

Nessa tilted her head. "Do you ever feel it, Detective? The darkness, curling at the edges of everything? It rides the mist. You can't always see it, but it is there. People think they understand this town, but they don't. Not really."

Claire took a grounding breath, refusing to be drawn into Nessa's cryptic monologue. "Nessa, we need you to explain why you have been around Lena's routes and near the scenes connected to the others. These are not coincidences."

Nessa's smile faded, and a strange sadness appeared. "Victor, arrogant, always trying to bend things to his will. I warned him once, you know. I told him that this town does not bow to anyone. He didn't listen."

She paused, distant now, somewhere far from the damp path and the present moment.

"Victor once told me that without structure, a rider is just spinning wheels. But he never stopped to ask who built the road beneath them."

Her voice was calm, but there was something frayed underneath. "He thought he was shaping the future. And maybe he was. But he didn't see how many people he was stepping over to get there. How many voices he silenced by pushing forward without waiting for them to catch up."

She blinked slowly, the moment slipping past, and then her tone shifted again.

"And Elliot," her words grew softer. "Young, brash, reckless. He laughed at the darkness and thought it was a game. You don't mock the shadows, Detective. Not if you want to keep them at bay."

She hesitated, the silence tightening between them.

"He flew down hills like fear was behind him, but it was always inside. That is the thing about people like Elliot. They ride hard so no one sees what is chasing them."

Ben cautiously took a step forward. "And what about Megan? Or Derek? And Jacob? What did they do to warrant your attention?"

Nessa's look carried a piercing edge, her expression impossible to read. "They were intruders. Megan with her softness, Derek with his rigidity, Jacob with his endless hunger for more. They forgot the boundaries, the lines between what is meant to be seen and what is meant to be left alone."

A wave of discomfort passed through Claire. The way Nessa spoke of the victims, the way she seemed to see them as symbols rather than people, was both unsettling and strangely revealing.

"Nessa, you are talking in circles. We need to know if you are responsible for what has been happening. If you know anything about the broken spokes left at each scene."

Nessa drifted, seeming to lose herself as she stared at her porch. "The broken spokes," she murmured. "They are reminders, Detective. Reminders of how easily things fall apart. Havenport has a history, a darkness woven into its bones. Some people think they can change it, bend it to their will."

Claire shivered. "Are you saying these murders are a part of that darkness? That the broken spokes are symbols?"

"Symbols, yes," Nessa said, a faint curve on her lips. "But they are more like tokens left behind for those who know how to look. The spokes mark the ones who thought they were untouchable. Those who believed the wheels would never turn on them. The road remembers, Detective. It never forgets."

Ben's voice broke. "Is that why you have been watching Lena? Because you think she has crossed a line?"

Nessa shifted to him. "Lena is young, full of fire. She rides like she owns the world, like nothing can touch her. She doesn't understand. Some things are older and darker than she could ever imagine. I watch her to remind her. To show her that no one is truly safe from what hides in the dark."

What followed was charged with an unspoken menace that hung between them. Nessa's words were maddeningly vague and full of symbolism. Yet her tone was sincere, a conviction that didn't waver.

"Nessa, if you know something, if there is any truth to what you are saying, you need to tell us. Are you involved in these deaths, or are you covering for someone?"

Nessa softened, pity crossing her face. "Covering," she repeated softly. "No, Detective. I am witness to the darkness that clings to this town. I have seen it consume people, swallowing them whole. You think you are close to the truth, but you don't understand."

"You're saying this is inevitable," Claire asked. "That there is no one to blame?"

Nessa's smile was sad and twisted. "Some things can't be stopped, Detective. They are as old as the roots of these trees, as deep as the silence beneath the waves. You can chase the fog all you want; you will never catch it. By the time you see what it truly holds, it is already too late."

With that, she stepped back into her house, the door closing softly behind her.

As they walked to the car, dread settled over Claire. Nessa's words lingered, carrying warnings that felt both ancient and personal. It was as if she had brushed against something older and darker than she could understand.

Ben turned toward her. "Did she just confess, Claire? I can't tell if she's responsible or if she truly believes she is an observer in all of this."

Claire stared off, her mind racing. "I don't know, Ben. But whatever this is, it is bigger than we realized. I think we are only beginning to understand the depths of what lies hidden here."

As evening deepened, Liam worked alone in the office, sur-rounded by the hum of old fluorescent lights and the comfort-ing chaos of his notes. The town outside was dark. A reminder of how long he had been at this, piecing together fragments of stories, memories, and whispers, all leading back to the same name. Marissa.

The word hung on his page. Her name sat at the center of it all, a thread connecting each victim in ways that became visible once he stepped back to look at the whole messy tapestry of her life.

He flipped through his notes on each victim. The years of tangled relationships that had drawn them together, their shared history within the cycling community. There was no denying that Marissa had once been at the heart of it all, until the accident. It had changed her life, pulling her out of the community she loved and leaving her isolated, bitter, and haunted by what she had lost.

Liam's pen tapped thoughtfully on his notebook as he considered the deeper layers of her resentment. Marissa had been more than a cyclist. She had been a rising star, a force within the local cycling world. Her accident had stolen that future from her. What had come after was, perhaps, even more painful. As her friends and rivals moved on, she had been left behind.

It was not only bitterness, Liam realized. It was a sense of betrayal. Her life had become an empty shell of what it could have been. Each victim represented a part of Marissa's fractured past, pieces of her former life that she could not reclaim.

As he sat there, the conclusion hit him. He knew he was onto the truth, buried beneath layers of resentment and regret. The air tonight was thick with unease, something he couldn't name. He edged closer to a threat just beginning to take shape.

Liam's fingers hovered over his keyboard as he began drafting his article, his heart racing with the thrill of the discovery. He would not write it yet. He needed more time, more proof. The outlines of his story were taking shape, and Marissa seemed more entangled in suspicion

.

He typed his words, capturing the duality of Marissa's fall from grace and the darkness that now seemed to surround her. "Once a rising talent, her promising career was stolen in the blink of an eye. But what if the resentment left in its wake has turned deadly?"

He paused, staring at the screen, feeling the gravity of his own words. Part of him wanted to reach out to Claire and Ben, to share what he had found, to warn them. He hesitated, uncertain of how they would react. Their attention was on Nessa and her open disdain for the cycling community.

Liam believed he knew better. Nessa was the illusion, the distraction. Marissa was the one who had suffered, the one whose life had been torn apart, who had retreated to the edges of the community she had once loved. She was the hidden force, the slow-burning resentment left to smolder too long.

As he leaned away, the faint sounds of the building settled through the office walls. Somewhere, a dog barked. The clock on the wall ticked steadily, marking the passing time. There was no urgency in Liam, no pressure to hand over his findings tonight. This was his story, his discovery.

He turned to his notebook, penning the final lines of his notes for the night.

Marissa is not angry. She has been watching, waiting, and now she is telling her story through each victim, each mark she has left behind.

The truth hit hard, leaving behind a cold unease he could not push away. He closed his notebook, his fingers brushing over the cover, as though he could trap the darkness within its pages.

Tomorrow, Liam told himself, he would look deeper and find the final pieces. The ones that would either prove his theory right or unravel it completely. For now, he let the silence fold around him, a comfort and a cage at once.

19

Broken Ends

The police station was hushed; a silence filled the air as Claire and Ben pored over their evidence. The recent reports about Nessa's strange behavior around town, her fixation on places tied to the victims, and her constant remarks about the fog and darkness had become impossible to ignore. Claire's instincts kept gnawing at her, suggesting there was a missing piece they hadn't uncovered.

Ben set down the file he was reading, looking up at Claire with a thoughtful frown. "We're getting close to needing a warrant, Claire. Everything's pointing at her, or at least close enough for a search. If we're going to make any headway in this case, we need to find a solid link between her and the victims."

Claire hesitated as she considered their next move. "I know, but it feels risky. We're working off suspicion, patterns, and cryptic comments she's made. What if we're wrong? A search warrant is invasive. It's crossing a line we can't uncross."

Ben nodded, sensing the force behind her words. Nessa had always existed on the fringes. Strange, yes, but never dangerous. She was a loner, not a lawbreaker. To bring a warrant against her meant disrupting her life, upending the fragile balance she'd maintained. Yet the evidence was stacking up against her, creating a path they could no longer ignore.

Claire spoke. "Let's gather what we have and run it by Judge Simmons. He's familiar with Nessa and the community, and he'll understand the gravity of this. If he agrees, then at least we know we're acting on solid ground."

Ben agreed, and together they carefully assembled the evidence to justify their request. They laid out reports from witnesses who had seen Nessa near the crime scenes and described the unsettling way she seemed to haunt Lena's usual routes.

There were accounts from townsfolk about Nessa's disdain for cyclists, along with the unsettling comments about secrets hidden in the stillness. They included details from her conversations with Claire, in which she'd hinted at knowing more than she was willing to say.

Each piece of evidence was troubling. As they reviewed it together, it became clear that while circumstantial, the growing gravity of it painted a disturbing picture.

With the paperwork assembled, they made their way to Judge Simmons's chambers. The judge was known for his fair and stern approach. He didn't give warrants lightly. Especially in cases involving individuals who, while eccentric, hadn't been proven dangerous. The severity of the situation, however, wasn't lost on him. His expression shifted from curiosity to suspicion as he reviewed the evidence.

Judge Simmons adjusted his glasses, his tone firm. "You're asking me to approve a search warrant for a woman who's lived here for decades without so much as a speeding ticket. Someone who's withdrawn from the community, not threatened it. I need more than unease. I need something solid."

Claire took a deep breath, collecting herself before speaking. "We understand, your Honor. We're not here because she's strange or reclusive. Nessa has exhibited behavior that aligns with traits we've seen before. Keeping herself on the outskirts, knowing details she shouldn't, openly stating her disdain for the victims' community. Her fixation on the victims' habits, the way she hangs around their usual routes. It's all building up to a concerning picture."

Ben leaned forward. "We're concerned there might be physical evidence linking her to the victims. Items she may have kept as a reminder of her actions. We can't move forward without knowing what she might be hiding in her home. We wouldn't ask this if we didn't feel it was necessary."

Judge Simmons watched them carefully. "I understand your concern. Remember, if you go into her home and find nothing, you will have stripped away the privacy of a reclusive woman who has spent her life keeping to herself. She's as much a part of this town as anyone else. If she's innocent, she will have to live with this breach of trust, knowing her community saw her as a threat."

Claire nodded. "We're aware of the risk, Your Honor. But if there's a chance she's involved, we can't ignore it. The victims deserve answers, and so does this town."

Judge Simmons sighed, tapping his pen thoughtfully against the desk before signing the paperwork. He handed them the warrant.

"Then I trust you'll be thorough and respectful. And remember, detectives, that finding evidence in her home doesn't necessarily mean she's the culprit. Be cautious. This case is more tangled than any I've seen in a long time."

With the signed warrant in hand, Claire and Ben left the Judge's chambers, the significance of the decision pressing down on them. Their confidence was tempered with a concern that followed as they returned to the station to prepare for the search. They knew that what lay ahead could either bring them closer to the truth or lead them down a path that would shake them to the core.

The air pressed tightly around Nessa Greene's cabin. Claire and Ben approached with the warrant in hand, aware that this could be the turning point in their case. The house, dark and unwelcoming, lay before them.

Claire knocked firmly. After a long pause, the door creaked

open, and Nessa appeared. She remained composed, a faint smile playing on her lips.

"Detective," she greeted. "Here to step into the darkness, are we?"

"We're here on official business, Nessa," Claire showed her the warrant. She was firm and respectful. "We have a warrant to search your property."

Nessa studied the document before she gave a slow, deliberate nod. "Then by all means," she stepped aside with a graceful sweep of her hand. "Come in. I hope you find what you're looking for, though I doubt you'll understand what it truly means."

Claire exchanged a look with Ben as they crossed the threshold into the dimly lit house. Inside, the air was stifling and tinged with the faint smell of turpentine and oil paint. Nessa's home was cluttered with canvases bearing dark, abstract images, twisted shapes that clung to the walls, their outlines warping beneath the weak light.

They began their search, moving through the house methodically. Careful not to disturb more than was necessary. Claire's flashlight illuminated shelves filled with strange knick-knacks and well-worn books on obscure subjects, each one covered in a thin layer of dust.

Then, in the back room, Ben's light caught a glint. "Claire, over here."

Claire joined him in what appeared to be Nessa's art studio, a room crowded with easels, paint-streaked rags, and brushes, all arranged with an obsessive precision. It was the wooden box that caught their attention. It was tucked partly under a stack of canvases, its polished surface gleaming faintly in the light.

Ben lifted the lid of the box, the cardboard creaking under the strain. Claire leaned in, both bracing for whatever they were about to find. Inside was a collection of personal items, neatly arranged, each one telling a story that neither of them could ignore.

Ben reached in first, carefully lifting out a worn leather wristband. Victor's initials were stamped into the faded band; the stitching frayed. Claire swallowed hard as Ben set it aside.

Next was a cracked bike headlight. Ben turned it over in his palm, wiping at the smudge on the lens with his thumb. "This was Elliot's," Claire nodded in agreement. Elliot always used an older model light and swore by it. There was a sticker on the underside, half-peeled, from a shop Elliot used to frequent. No question it was his.

Claire reached in this time and pulled out a dented stainless-steel water bottle. Megan Sharpe's name was scrawled across it in permanent marker, faded but still clear. She had carried it everywhere, even when she wasn't on her bike. It had been missing since the day they found her body.

Ben's hand moved toward a small, battered paperback. A

cycling manual. Dog-eared and marked up. He flipped it open and scanned the notes scribbled in the margins. "This was Derek's," he said. The handwriting matched the notebooks they'd found at his place. Derek had treated that book like a bible.

Then came Jacob's race tag. A cold wave swept through Claire as she ran her thumb over the weathered paper. His number from last year's Classic was printed in bold black ink. It shouldn't be here.

Without a word, they sat together, fixed on the items laid out before them like offerings at an altar. Claire drew a slow breath and reached deeper into the box. What she found next made her blood run cold.

A rusted chain link from an old bike lock. Heavy, cold, and stiff with age. On one of the links was an engraved initial: *D.F.* Darren Fletcher. Claire's pulse jumped.

Ben pulled out a cracked helmet visor next, cloudy with age. Inside the rim, faint handwriting spelled out a name: *M. Travers.* Michael Travers.

At the very bottom of the box, Claire found a thin silver bracelet with a single charm shaped like a wheel. She ran her fingers over the worn surface, recognizing it immediately from the old photos of Danica Shaw. After Danica's death, her family had asked about it, but it was never recovered, until now.

Claire laid it out in front of them, next to the others, a strange sense of ceremony to it.

"These aren't trophies," she murmured, her throat tight. "They're personal. Intimate." She glanced at Ben. "She's been holding onto them for years."

Ben stared at the row of items, his expression darkening. "That's a dark history in one box."

Claire shifted towards Nessa, who had followed them silently into the room. She stood by the door with an unsettling calm as she watched them examine her collection.

"You're wondering why I have these things." Her voice was calm, almost detached. "I've been keeping pieces of them. Fragments. Reminders of the lives that brush against the edge. Havenport is... selective, Detective. It decides who belongs and who doesn't."

Claire chose her words carefully. "Nessa, these items connect you to the victims. They're not reminders; they are meaningful possessions. We need you to come with us."

A look of tragic understanding crossed her face. "I knew you'd come. The fog whispers, you know, tells me when the time is near."

She peeked at the box, her expression bittersweet. "You think this is about them, but they were offerings, reminders of the cost of living in the light."

Ben stepped forward. "We must take you into custody, Nessa. We need to understand how you came to possess these items, how deeply you're connected to the lives that were lost."

Nessa studied both of them, her face unreadable. Then, with a small, resigned sigh, she held out her hands, a faint smile tugging at her lips.

"Very well. Remember, detectives, Havenport has layers, deeper than you can see, older than you can know. You can look at these things all you want. You won't find what's hidden beneath."

As they led her outside, the mist wrapped around them. Nessa walked with calm dignity. Her expression distant and dream-like. The world narrowed as she climbed into the cruiser, her face composed yet tinged with a darkness she couldn't hide.

Claire climbed into the driver's seat, glancing at Ben as he slid in beside her. In the rearview mirror, Nessa's eyes met Claire's, a shiver crawling down her spine. As they drove to the station, Claire's mind turned with questions, each one twisting deeper into the darkness. The evidence was clear, damning even.

Nessa's arrest had rippled through the town, unsettling it in ways few could put into words. Even in custody, her cryptic words and unnerving calm left a lasting mark on those who knew of her deep disdain for cyclists and her fixation on the shadows.

Though many shared a sense of relief, the town remained

subdued, not yet convinced the nightmare was over. Lena sensed it too, though she couldn't explain why. She'd tossed and turned in bed, unable to shake the images of Nessa and the items found in her home. The trophies that spoke of lives cut short.

By morning, Lena couldn't bear the restless unease gnawing at her any longer and decided to head out on a ride, hoping that the familiar rhythm of her tires on asphalt might calm her nerves. As she started down the road, she kept telling herself that Nessa's arrest should bring her peace. That the woman responsible for so much fear in the cycling community was behind bars.

Lena pressed forward, her legs pumping harder as she guided her bike along the winding, narrow road. She swallowed, her mouth dry as a sense of being watched washed over her, prickling her skin despite the crisp morning air.

As she rounded the corner, where twisted branches draped the road, the feeling grew stronger. An unseen presence followed, hidden in the thick brush or behind the gnarled trunks of ancient trees. Her breath quickened, and she forced herself to keep looking forward, resisting the urge to turn around.

She sped up, her tires cutting through the thin layer of moisture on the road, the sound barely enough to drown out the eerie silence surrounding her. As she rode through another darkened stretch of road, the feeling continued to grow. It was more than nerves, more than the lasting effects of the past few weeks. She could feel it. Something, someone, was there, hovering on the edge.

In a flash, she glanced over her shoulder, her heart pounding as she searched the road behind her. There was nothing but the swirling gray. Lena shivered, her hands gripping the handlebars tightly as she tried to calm herself, telling herself that it was paranoia. A trick of her imagination.

Each darkened corner she neared grew heavier than the last, daring her to step deeper. She told herself to keep going, to push through. Her senses remained alert, her heart hammering as she rounded the final bend toward town.

The air cleared, giving way to the faint lights and the welcoming glow of the Haven Café up ahead. The sight was a relief, yet a small part of her couldn't ignore the haunting presence that lingered behind her.

She slowed as she approached the café, stopping and dismounting her bike. Her pulse racing, she leaned her bike against the rack and stood there. Breathing deeply, she let the warmth of the café's lights ease the chill.

She paused outside the Haven Café, feeling the warmth from its glowing windowsill. She could hear the low hum of voices inside, sharper and more agitated than usual. News of Nessa's arrest had made its way through town. The café was packed with regulars. They whispered to each other, stirred by the shock of what had happened.

Taking a deep breath, Lena stepped inside. The usual morning calm gave way to a restless buzz as people leaned in close over steaming mugs. Their faces filled with a mixture of shock, relief, and disbelief.

Marie was moving from table to table, refilling coffee cups and offering a calming presence as people processed the news. Lena took a seat near the window, her gaze drifting over the familiar faces in the crowd.

"Should've seen this coming," an elderly man at a nearby table muttered, shaking his head. "All those years, Nessa acting strange, muttering about cyclists like they were vermin."

Across from him, a woman who'd been a longtime friend of the community folded her arms tightly. "Strange, yes," she replied, her tone skeptical. "But a murderer? That's something else entirely. She's been a part of this town forever. Maybe she's odd, but I can't picture her going that far."

Lena glanced down, guilt rising in her chest. Like so many others, she had dismissed Nessa's words and strange ways, brushing them off as quirks rather than threats.

Across the room, she spotted Ryan sitting alone by the window. His expression held more than relief. When Lena caught his eye, he gave her a small, tired nod as she walked over.

"Mind if I join you?" she asked.

"Please," he said, gesturing to the seat across from him.

Lena slid into the chair, nodding once before wrapping her hands around the warmth of the mug in front of her. She studied him for a moment. The fatigue wasn't just physical, it was deep.

"Hard to believe it's over," she said before taking a sip of her coffee.

Ryan nodded, his fingers tapping against the tabletop. "Yeah," he said after a moment. "Everyone's acting like we're safe again. Like we just hit reset."

He peered out the window, where the street buzzed with cautious optimism. People were beginning to smile again, to let their guard down.

"I don't know how to do that," he said. "I don't even remember what normal was supposed to feel like."

Lena shifted slightly, watching him. Months ago, she might've brushed off his words. Not anymore.

"I don't think we're supposed to go back," she said. "Not after something like this."

He looked at her, waiting.

"We lived through it," she continued. "That doesn't make us stronger. It just means we're still here. And that's not the same thing."

Ryan let the thought settle. "I keep thinking about why. Why us? Why did we walk away when they didn't?"

Lena gave a slight shake of her head. "There's no logic in it. No clean reason. I've gone over it a hundred times, and it never adds up."

Ryan's voice lowered. "Still… it's hard not to notice how it always seemed to come back around. Like the town would forget just long enough, and then…"

He trailed off, and she didn't press.

"I still hear them," he said after a moment. "It's like they're frozen in time. Their voices, their laughs, the way they rode."

Lena's voice softened. "I used to think healing meant forgetting. Now I think it just means learning how to carry it differently."

He looked at her, the edge of something easing in his expression. "You really believe that?"

"I'm starting to," she said.

Lena spoke again, slower now. "Have you heard what people are saying about Nessa?"

Ryan's mouth tightened. "Bits and pieces. That they found things at her place. Things that tie her to it all."

"Whatever that means," Lena said. She traced her finger along the edge of her mug. "It's all so vague, but the town seems satisfied. Like naming her closed the door on it."

"She never made it easy on herself," Ryan muttered. "Always glaring at us on the road. Muttering. That weird way she'd show up without warning. It's like everyone's collecting those memories now and twisting them into proof."

Lena nodded. "She hated us. We knew that. But hate alone doesn't explain everything."

"You think she didn't do it?" he asked, not accusing, just open.

"I don't know," Lena admitted. "I want to believe it's over. I really do. But it's hard to shake the way it... repeated."

Ryan leaned forward, elbows on the table. "Maybe that's just what fear does; makes patterns out of shadows."

"Maybe," she said quietly.

Outside, someone laughed. A bike rolled past the window, the whirr of its wheels blending into the background hum of the café.

For a moment, neither of them spoke. The silence felt lighter than before.

Across town, suspicion hung in the Police Department. Claire and Ben sat side by side, surrounded by the evidence they had painstakingly gathered.

"Nessa hated cyclists, Claire. Everyone knew it. She practically spat on them whenever they rode by. I'm not surprised she'd go this far. I mean, look at this evidence."

He pointed to the collection they'd found in her home. "She kept these pieces as souvenirs. It feels... compulsive, doesn't it? Even unhinged."

Claire nodded, though her expression remained contemplative. "I know, Ben. Nessa wasn't angry with cyclists on the roads; she had deep personal resentment. It was as if they were taunting her every time they sped by. Flaunting their freedom while she remained on the outskirts, literally and figuratively."

She leaned away. "Keeping these items so close... It's like she wanted us to find them."

Ben tilted his head, picking up on the undertone of doubt. "Do you think she's capable of that kind of manipulation? Keeping these items in plain sight, only to make herself look suspicious?"

Claire weighed the possibilities. "Maybe. Or maybe it's compulsive behavior. She could keep them because they symbolize her control over these cyclists. Her way of holding onto them, even in death." She hesitated, glancing at Ben.

"But then, there's a calculated edge to it all. A woman like Nessa, angry? Yes. Obsessive? Definitely. But could she orchestrate this?"

Ben frowned. "It's easy to want it to be convenient, Claire. Let's look at the facts. All the evidence suggests she was the one behind each death. We know she was out there, lurking, at odd hours, near their routes. If we hadn't caught her when we did, she would have struck again."

"Yeah," Claire agreed, "she was close enough to know their habits, to track their routes."

There was a knock. Claire looked up from the timeline spread across the table as Liam stepped into the doorway.

"I won't stay long," he said. "But I've got something I think you should see."

Claire exchanged a glance with Ben. "If this is another theory…"

"It's not," Liam cut in gently. "I'm not here to speculate."

Claire folded her arms but gave a nod. "Then say what you came to say."

Liam stepped forward and laid a slim folder on the edge of the table. "People have been talking to me. Not big statements, just observations. Things they didn't think mattered at the time. A couple patterns caught my attention. Overlapping routes. Schedule changes. Shifts in habits right before the attacks."

Ben remained seated, his expression unreadable. "You're aware we can't discuss anything related to the investigation."

"I'm not asking you to," Liam replied. "And I'm not publishing anything based on this. Not yet. But I thought you should see it in case it supports something you already know."

"Why bring it here and not run with it?" she asked.

Liam hesitated. "Because the towns already made up its mind. Nessa's guilt fits what they want to believe. If I run something now, I risk feeding that. Or worse, pointing fingers without proof."

Ben leaned forward. "So, what do you want from us?"

"Nothing," Liam said. "Not officially. I just want to make sure you have everything that might help. And, if you're willing, I'd like to include a line in the piece I'm working on. Something about the investigation remaining open to follow-up leads. Not stir anything, just to keep the story accurate."

Claire studied him for a long moment. "No names. No theories."

"None," Liam said. "It's a story about what happens to a place when the threat seems over. What people let themselves believe. I'm not here to second-guess your case. I'm just saying, if there's even a sliver of something else out there, I'd rather not help bury it."

Claire opened the folder and scanned the top page; quick field notes, timestamps, and a few names she recognized. No claims or accusations. Just community noise arranged into something more watchful.

Ben looked at Claire. "We don't act on whispers."

"No," she said. "But sometimes whispers point you back to the thing you missed."

She closed the folder and set it aside. "You can say the department is reviewing all relevant information. Nothing more."

Liam nodded. "Fair."

He paused. "And if anything in there crosses a line, tell me. I'll hold it."

Claire offered a faint nod. "Appreciated."

As he turned to go, Liam hesitated. "I know I've been a pain in your side. I just... I want to get this one right."

Ben said nothing, but Claire replied. "So do we."

Liam left quickly, the door clicking shut behind him. Claire stood still for a moment, then turned back toward the table.

Ben leaned forward, arms on the table. "You think he's right? That we've missed something?"

Claire glanced toward the evidence board. The lines were all drawn, the conclusions clean.

"Everything fits," she said. "But maybe that's what keeps me up at night."

20

Out of the Shadows

Claire sat in her living room; legs tucked beneath her on the edge of the couch. Her coffee had gone cold. Across from it sat Liam's file, still neatly stacked. The room was silent except for the hum of the fridge and the tick of the wall clock, sounds that felt too loud.

She reached forward and flipped the file open. Names she had seen before. Notes she recalled. A town mapped through whispers and fragments. Then, tucked halfway through the stack, she caught a line she did not remember reading.

A neighbor's comment: *Used to keep an old black bike locked in the shed. Said it was for storms only.*

Claire's fingers stopped. Her mind flashed to the photograph from Nessa's cabin: a younger version of Nessa with dust on her cheeks, grinning beside another woman. Behind them, the ridgeline, the curve of pavement, and the faint blur of a warning sign near the quarry. The black bike, the photograph, and the broken spoke. Her stomach tightened as she reached for her phone.

"Ben. Meet me at her house. Bring gloves."

A short time later, they stood outside the shed. Claire stepped through first, Ben following behind her, their flashlights slicing through the dim air. The space smelled of rust and pine sap, as though the forest had begun to reclaim it.

"There," Claire said.

It was tucked in the far corner, barely visible under an old tarp. A matte black frame with no reflectors. Chain clean, tires full. Someone had cared for it recently. Ben crouched near the rear wheel and ran his fingers along the spokes.

"This one's new. Replaced clean."

Claire didn't move. Her gaze followed the faint path leading away from the shed through the trees. Worn grass and scuffed dirt. She already knew where it ended. The quarry. They left without another word.

The holding room at the station felt colder than usual. Nessa sat alone at the table, hands folded. The room hummed faintly. Claire stepped in and placed a small evidence bag on the table. Inside was a single broken spoke.

Nessa didn't move.

Claire sat down across from her. "That photograph in your cabin. The one near the quarry. That was the loop, wasn't it. You rode it. You both did."

Nessa's eyes stayed fixed on the spoke. Her voice was low and almost absent.

"We rode it before the maps. Before it had a name. Back when it was just the road, the silence, and the promise of something wild. It was ours."

Claire stayed still, watching her. There was a tremor beneath Nessa's calm, a hairline crack in the armor she had worn for years.

"She went down near the quarry," Nessa said. "Took the bend too fast. Loose gravel. The spoke had already started to split. I knew it before we left." Her mouth twitched.

"I told her it could hold."

"You kept the bike," Claire said quietly.

"The one we built together. We welded every joint. Tuned the frame to the curves of that loop."

Nessa's eyes moved to the narrow window high on the wall where no real light came through.

"After she died, the others returned, louder and faster. Coating the road in neon. Their laughter cut through the stillness like it had never swallowed anyone."

She looked at Claire now, something fierce and hollow stirring in her expression. "They forgot her."

Claire's fingers tightened around her pen. She thought of Victor's control, Elliot's recklessness, Megan's fragile hope, Derek's rigid order, Jacob's steady comfort. And Ryan, standing where all their pieces met, surviving out of sheer defiance. They had been the load-bearing beams of this town. And Nessa had been pulling them out one by one.

"You helped with the routes and the trails?" Claire asked, her voice low.

"For a year," Nessa said. "I thought if I stayed close, maybe I could hold it all together. Honor what was left."

She paused, her voice thinning. "But the noise never stopped. They didn't stop."

"And then?"

"Then came the silence. And the silence broke."

"The five-year pattern?"

"Not a pattern. A tide," Nessa murmured. "Grief. Then pressure. Then something cracked inside me, just like that spoke. And it never healed."

Claire reached for the bag. The spoke lay cold and coiled, as if memory itself had hardened inside it.

Nessa's gaze followed it. "They were not warnings. They were keepsakes. Each one held what they refused to see. The flaw in their speed. The crack in their certainty. The spoke was not a threat. It was the proof."

Claire's voice softened. "You were the Ghost Rider."

Nessa turned back to the window, her voice thinning to a whisper. "They only saw speed, sweat, and finish lines. But I saw what was lost in the silence between spokes. I saw her, every time. The way she hit the ground. The way the world went quiet around her name."

Claire sat with it, not pity, not forgiveness, only the ache of understanding.

Nessa leaned back, eyes closing. "That is enough now."

Claire rose slowly, gathering the bagged spoke. She paused at the door, looking back one last time. Nessa did not open her eyes.

Outside the room, the corridor felt colder. Ben waited near his office, one hand on the doorframe as if he had been holding up the building. He studied Claire's face, then stepped aside to let her in. The blinds were half drawn, the desk a mess of reports and unanswered calls. Claire set the bag in the corner and sat.

"She confessed," Ben said.

"She told the truth she believes." Claire rubbed her temples, then dropped her hands. "It was grief that curdled. Precision dressed as fate."

Ben lowered into his chair. "You pushed it over the line. In the right way."

"She would have kept going," Claire said. "Maybe not tomorrow. Maybe not for another season. But she would have."

Ben nodded, then looked at the bag. "You carried this for all of us. I did not make it easier."

"You kept me steady. Even when you thought I might be wrong." Claire's mouth tightened. "I was afraid of missing it. Afraid of repeating old mistakes."

Ben's expression shifted, softer. "You didn't miss."

They sat quietly. Outside, the station door opened and closed, footsteps coming and going, the normal rhythms returning. Ben leaned forward, elbows on his knees.

"Take the rest of today," he said. "File what you need. Then go home, Claire."

She stood. "I will file it now."

He reached for the bag, then let his hand fall. "I will call the commissioner."

Claire picked up the spoke again and left the office. She could feel the weight of the day settling along her shoulders.

Outside the station, reporters had begun to cluster on the steps, murmuring like gulls before a storm. Ben stood at the edge of the lot, his arm around his niece's shoulders. She leaned into him, her bike helmet dangling loosely from her hand. Her eyes were red but dry, her face pale beneath freckles.

"Are they really done?" she whispered.

Ben hesitated, then pulled her into a firmer hug. "Yeah," he said. "They are done." He kissed the top of her head, his voice breaking just slightly. "And you are staying off those roads at dawn. Deal?"

She nodded against his coat. Claire passed them, saying nothing, but she caught Ben's grateful glance and nodded back. He had finally let the weight settle. So had she.

Across town, the Gazette office was nearly empty. Liam stared at his draft, the cursor blinking at a paragraph he had rewritten four times. He deleted it. The easy headline collapsed into dust. He thought of Nessa, the spoke, and the way fear had wrapped itself around the town.

He typed, slower now, choosing care over spectacle: *Grief left its shadow on Havenport, and for a while we mistook it for a ghost. It was only us, riding too fast to see what we had lost along the way.* He read it once, then twice, then hit publish. He closed his laptop and sat in the lingering quiet, the newsroom finally breathing.

On the far side of Main, Marissa stood at the back of her shop, a wrench still in her hand though she was not doing much with it. Dust hung like quiet around her. She heard the door creak and did not need to turn.

"I figured you would come," she said.

Ryan stepped in, brushing a speck of grit from his jacket. "Was not sure if I should."

"Then why did you."

He exhaled and glanced around the room. The old race photos. The shelf with a bent trophy he had teased her about once, long ago. The scuffed floor where she had paced after the crash, refusing to sit because sitting made it too real.

"Because I didn't want it to end like this. With everything hanging in the air. You and me. This place. Nessa."

Marissa leaned against the workbench, setting the wrench down. "You were always the one who needed resolution."

"And you were always the one who knew when to walk away," Ryan said gently. "Or maybe you just learned to stop needing people to understand you."

She gave a faint smile. "Maybe. Or I just stopped hoping they would."

He stepped closer, not too close. "Back then, I thought I knew what you needed. I thought loving you meant fixing everything."

"And I thought silence would protect me," she said. "It didn't."

Ryan nodded slowly. "We both disappeared. Just in different ways."

Marissa's gaze fell to the trophy. "Do you remember the hill out on Red Pine."

"The one you swore would make me quit."

"You flew down it the first time," she said, a small laugh catching. "I pretended I wasn't impressed."

"I was terrified," he said. "You knew."

"I always knew." She lifted her eyes. "I stayed because I had to. Because leaving would have meant it was all gone. But it wasn't. Not entirely."

"You survived," he said softly.

"I adapted."

The quiet remained, not painful, just fragile. Ryan walked to the wall of spare parts and trailed his fingers along a hook of unused chains. He looked smaller in the shop than he used to.

"I'm leaving town for a bit," he said. "Maybe longer. I need distance."

She did not ask where. She reached out and touched his arm. "Take care of yourself, Ryan. Stop trying to carry everything for everyone else."

"I will try." He started for the door, paused, then looked back. "I did love you, you know. Back then."

Marissa's gaze stayed steady. "I know."

He nodded once and left; the bell above the door giving a single ring.

Claire was just passing as Ryan stepped out. They almost collided on the sidewalk.

"Hey," he said quietly.

"Hey."

"I heard about Nessa."

Claire nodded, her face unreadable.

"It is done," he asked.

"It is done," she said, though the words scraped like gravel. "It is done."

Ryan studied her. "Are you okay."

"I don't know."

"You don't have to be. Not yet."

They stood together in the hush of the street, the town finally still. A gull cried once over the harbor and the sound fell away. Ryan looked as if he might say something and then didn't.

"I need to get out of here for a while," he said. "But I will come back. If you want me to."

Claire met his eyes. Something in her finally softened. "If you come back," she said, "I will be here."

Ryan's lips curved faintly. "Good."

He reached up, gently brushing her hair behind her ear like he had once before, back when everything was chaos. This time, she did not flinch. She stepped closer.

The kiss was slow, uncertain, then steady. It was not fiery, it was real. The kind of kiss that carried everything unsaid but understood. When they parted, neither spoke. Ryan touched her hand lightly, then walked off down the quiet street, his figure fading into the light fog.

Later that night, Lena rode. The roads were empty, still holding the ghost of cheering voices. Her tires whispered over damp pavement, each turn of the pedals pushing back the fear that had followed her for weeks.

The air was sharp, clean. She found a rhythm she didn't have to force. She passed Millie's dark windows and caught her own reflection moving smooth and constant, a shape that looked like herself again.

At the ridge she stopped, the sea spread below, dark and endless. For the first time in days, her hands didn't shake. She wasn't riding to win. She was riding to belong again. She clipped in, pushed off, and let the road carry her forward.

Near midnight, Claire returned home. The house was dark and quiet. She hung her coat and pulled the broken spoke from her pocket. It lay cold in her hand, its edges dulled by time and grief. It was not a clue or a weapon. It was what remained after the fear burned away.

She set it on the table and stood for a moment with her palms pressed to the wood, listening to the soft creak of the house around her. The darkness was not something to fear now. It was simply where the light had not reached.

She turned from the spoke and walked down the hall, steady and unhurried, leaving the shadows behind.

About the Author

Jody Savage is a writer and creator based on the coast of Maine. She crafts emotionally rich stories rooted in quiet towns, hidden histories, and the resilience of the human spirit. When she is not writing, she is building her creative brand, Motivated Savages, and exploring new ways to spark boldness in others. *Shadows on the Road* is her debut novel.

You can connect with me on:
🌐 https://motivatedsavages.com